P.C. Cast lives in Oklah... spoiled cat and her Scot... The daughter attends co... The Scottinators are as y...

New York Times and *US...*
Showalter has been pra... ...d
"utterly spellbinding stories". Readers can't get enough of her
trademark wit and singular imagination. To learn more about
Gena and her books, please visit www.genashowalter.com and
www.genashowalterblogspot.com.

Multiple *New York Times* bestseller **Maggie Shayne** is one of
the hottest authors currently writing paranormal romance.
Her works are fresh and sexy, carrying the reader into a darkly
compelling and fully realised world where vampires are
creatures of the heart, not just the night.

Rhyannon Byrd fell in love with a Brit whose accent was just
too sexy to resist. Luckily for her, he turned out to be a keeper,
so she married him and they now have two adorable children
who constantly keep her on her toes. When not writing,
Rhyannon loves to travel, lose herself in books and watch as
much football as humanly possible with her loud, fun-loving
family. For information on Rhyannon's books and the latest
news, you can visit her website—www.rhyannonbyrd.com.

P.C. CAST
GENA SHOWALTER
MAGGIE SHAYNE
RHYANNON BYRD

Darkness Divine

MIRA

All the characters in this book have no existence outside the imagination of the author, and have no relation whatsoever to anyone bearing the same name or names. They are not even distantly inspired by any individual known or unknown to the author, and all the incidents are pure invention.

First published in Great Britain 2010.
MIRA Books, Eton House, 18-24 Paradise Road,
Richmond, Surrey, TW9 1SR

© Harlequin Books S.A. 2010

Divine Beginnings © Harlequin Books S. A. 2007
The Amazon's Curse © Gena Showalter 2009
Voodoo © Harlequin Books S. A. 2001
Edge of Craving © Tabitha Bird 2009

ISBN 978 0 7783 0406 7

54-1010

MIRA's policy is to use papers that are natural, renewable and recyclable products and made from wood grown in sustainable forests. The logging and manufacturing processes conform to the legal environmental regulations of the country of origin.

Printed in Great Britain
by Clays Ltd, St Ives plc

Contents

Divine Beginnings

P.C. CAST

1

Aine liked the irony of using a funeral urn to draw water for the herbs in her healer's garden. It was a beautiful urn, large and graceful, with a ridged lip and a curved handle balanced off one side. The scene painted around it was framed in black, as was typical for Epona's funeral urns, but it seemed to Aine that there was something especially lovely about this one. The Goddess's Chosen reclined with her outstretched arm motioning regally to the line of supplicants that stretched around the urn before her. A riot of auburn hair cascaded like water down the priestess's back.

It was ridiculous that something so beautiful be relegated to the dreary job of pouring libations on graves, or worse, holding the ashes of the dead. So Aine had "rescued" it.

Too bad there would be no one to rescue her from the dreary job she'd taken.

"No," Aine muttered. "It's not the job that's dreary. It's the place." She sat at the edge of the herb bed and looked around her. She'd been at Guardian Castle for a little over five full turns of the moon, but she still wasn't used to the overwhelming grayness of everything. The castle was gray. The pass through the mountains the castle had been built within was gray. The autumn sky was gray. Aine sighed. "Epona's shield! Even the people are gray."

She understood that the castle had been built for one specific purpose: to keep the pass between the Wastelands and Partholon guarded so that the demonic Fomorians who had been banished to those Wastelands would never enter Partholon again. Even though there hadn't been a Fomorian sighted in generations, still they needed to be on guard. So beauty and color and the things that made Partholon such a lovely goddess-blessed land weren't exactly priorities here at the edge of the civilized world. Protection and defense was the focus.

It was just so hard to get used to this stark place

after four full seasons of studying the art of healing at the exquisite Temple of the Muse, where Aine had been surrounded by all the most talented, beautiful and brightest women of Partholon.

Camenae, her mentor, had warned her against accepting the austere post, but Aine had known that Guardian Castle was where she belonged. Just as she had known that it was her destiny to be a Healer.

But since Aine had arrived at Guardian Castle she'd felt so uneasy that she'd begun questioning that intuition, that *knowing* which had served her so well all her life. Restless, Aine picked at a few sprigs of mint, breathing deeply of the distinctive scent of the plant. She had to stop second guessing herself. It wasn't her intuition that was the problem. The problem was the people here. They felt wrong. They were as colorless, inside and out, as the landscape surrounding them.

Well, the human people that is. Aine had only made one friend since she'd taken up her position as Healer of Guardian Castle. She and the centaur Maev, who had only recently been posted as Huntress for the castle, had instantly clicked.

"Probably because we're the only bit of color hereabouts. Maybe that's why I believed so strongly that I needed to come here—to spread some color around."

Aine picked up a raven-colored curl that had fallen over her shoulder. She smiled as the wan sunlight made her hair shine with flashes of mahogany and a black so dark it almost appeared blue. With her dark hair and startlingly sapphire eyes, and Maev's blazing copper hair and shining roan equine coat, the two of them definitely stood out amongst the dish soap, milk toast complexions of the stone-faced warriors and their equally boring women.

It was just so odd. She'd had no idea before she'd arrived how washed out everything—every*one* would be. But then, why would the rest of Partholon know? Besides families of the warriors and a few traders, people rarely visited Guardian Castle.

Aine couldn't help but compare the people of Guardian Castle to sleepwalkers. Or worse—they were like the stories told to frighten children about people who had been led astray by darkness and who ended up wandering the earth as soulless husks eternally searching for but unable to ever find the light within them that had been bled away by…

"Aine! There has been an accident. You're needed!"

2

Aine startled at the appearance of the stern warrior she thought was called Edan, but she had been well trained and recovered quickly. She was on her feet and running for her Healer's basket in an instant. Then instead of heading to the infirmary wing of the castle, the warrior called, "This way!" and began jogging towards the massive rear gate that opened to the Wastelands side of the pass.

She stifled her questions, concentrating instead on keeping up with the silent warrior as they ran out the raised, iron-toothed gate.

The instant Aine passed beyond the walls of the castle she felt the change. It was as if the air had solidified. It pressed down upon her, thick…heavy…cloying… Aine stumbled.

Edan grabbed her arm to steady her. "We only have a short way to go." He jogged down the narrow, slate-colored pass. Aine rushed after him. The path took a sharp turn. Not far ahead of them Aine could see a warrior standing in front of a pile of something that was lying in the middle of the pass. She caught the scent of fresh blood and centered herself so that she would be calm and able to think clearly in the whirlwind of emotion and activity that accompanied injuries as surely as blood and death accompanied them.

The warrior turned to her and Aine looked beyond him to see—

"Maev!" She gasped and dropped to her knees beside the centaur Huntress, instantly assessing the gaping slash wounds that appeared to cover her body. Her friend was unconscious. Her breath was shallow and her skin, that which was not covered with blood, was so pale it appeared colorless.

"We found her like this. She was hunting wild boar today. One of the beasts must have attacked her," said the Warrior, pointing at the centaur's terrible wounds.

Aine glanced up at him. "She's been unconscious the whole time?"

"Yes."

"She needs to be moved to the infirmary." Aine snapped the order, the steadiness of her voice completely belying the tumult within her. "Get a stretcher and more men." Aine was vaguely aware that Edan nodded and rushed off. All of her attention was focused on her fallen friend as she pulled linen strips from her basket. She had to stop the bleeding. But there were so many wounds… so much blood lost.

Aine was leaning over the centaur's torso, pressing a linen cloth to the ripped flesh of her neck and trying to staunch the flood of her friend's lifeblood when Maev, eyes still closed, lips barely moving, whispered "Send him away."

Aine drew in a shocked breath, but before she could respond further, Maev's strained whisper continued. "Do not betray me."

Used to relying on her instincts, especially during emergencies, Aine made her decision quickly. She turned to the warrior. She didn't know his name, but she recognized his heavily lined face as one of the senior guards. "I'm going to have to close some of her wounds before we move her. I'll need everything in my large black surgical box in the infirmary." When the warrior didn't move, Aine lifted her chin and said, "Now."

Expressionless, the warrior hesitated for only a moment more before he turned and sprinted down the path towards the castle.

Maev's eyes opened instantly. "Must listen to me." The Huntress was growing weaker by the moment. She struggled to speak as the breath gurgled wetly in her throat.

Aine wanted to soothe her friend—to tell her to save her strength, but she'd already seen the end written in the color of Maev's skin and the copious amount of blood she'd lost. Even a centaur Huntress couldn't survive such terrible wounds.

"What is it, Maev?"

The centaur's eyes widened and she coughed, raining scarlet down her chest. "It —it's come here. The darkness…the claws and teeth in the darkness."

"Maev, I don't understand."

The Huntress gripped Aine's wrist. "Don't let my pyre be built here, or inside the walls of that tainted castle. Send me to Epona from the forest of Partholon."

"You're not going to die," Aine lied. "Rest now."

"Promise me!"

"Yes, of course, I promise." She soothed. "What did this to you, Maev?"

"The warriors know! They know."

"About what?"

"Fomorians." Maev spoke the name and then, as if the dreaded word had taken her soul with it, her eyes went wide and blank, and the Huntress died.

3

"You said a boar did this?" Numbly, Aine watched the warriors put Maev's body on the stretcher and carry her back to the castle.

Edan nodded. "Urien found the tracks of the beast not far down the pass. He said there were signs of a great battle between it and the Huntress."

Deep in thought, Aine followed the warriors and their bloody burden. Guardian Castle's Lord and Chieftain of Clan Monro met them at the rear gate.

"It is the Huntress," he sighed wearily and shook his head. "She was too young and inexperienced to tangle with a wounded boar."

"Those gashes don't look like any boar goring I've ever seen," Aine heard herself saying.

The Monro's sharp eyes locked on her. "Aine, is it? Our new Healer?"

She nodded. "Yes, my Lord." Aine had been presented to the Chieftain when she'd arrived, but their paths had rarely crossed since. Actually, this was the first opportunity she'd had to study the Monro closely and she was surprised by how gaunt and unhealthy he appeared. *A wasting sickness*…The thought had her pitying him. Until he spoke again.

"How many boar wounds have you tended?" His words were thick with sarcasm. "You couldn't save the centaur, could you?"

"No," she said softly. "I couldn't."

"It appears you're as young and inexperienced as she was. See that you come to a better end. Perhaps you should begin by leaving the details of hunting and such to those who are older and wiser." He turned his back on her and spoke to the warriors. "Send a runner to notify her herd, and then build a pyre near the burial mounds within the east wall. We will fire it on the morrow."

Aine drew a deep, fortifying breath and stepped in front of the Chieftain. "That's not what she wanted."

The Monro raised his brows at her. "Indeed?"

"Yes, my Lord, Maev asked that her pyre be built out there." Aine pointed towards the distant forest that spread south of the castle and marked the beginning of Partholon.

The Monro snorted. "Partholon is also within the walls of this castle."

Aine countered with, "She was a Huntress. She deserves to be sent to Epona from the forest."

The Monro shrugged. "It matters naught to me, but if it means so much to you, Healer, then you see to it. I'll not interfere."

It took the entire next day for Aine to prepare Maev's pyre. The Monro had been true to his word. He hadn't interfered with her. He also hadn't ordered any of the warriors to help her. At least Edan had aided her in loading and then unloading the cart with boughs for the fire. He'd also gathered enough warriors to carry Maev's body to the bier.

They hadn't liked that she'd picked a spot in the middle of a clearing that was quite a ways from the castle. Aine hadn't cared. She'd known Maev would have wanted to be far enough away so that the gloomy walls wouldn't be visible above the pines.

It was almost dusk when everything was ready. Aine faced the south—the direction of Partholon and the Centaur Plains beyond. She was nervous. A Shaman should be doing this, but there was no Shaman living at Guardian Castle and the taciturn warriors who stood restlessly beside her certainly weren't going to evoke the Goddess's blessing.

"Epona, centaur Huntress Maev of the Hagan Herd, was my friend. We laughed together a lot, even when things felt really grim. She died too soon and I'll miss her. I ask that you welcome her to your verdant meadows so that her spirit will gallop free by your side for eternity." She touched the torch to the pyre. With a *whoosh* the oil-soaked boughs caught fire.

Well done, daughter.

Aine jumped and gasped when the Goddess's sweet voice drifted through her mind.

And now prepare yourself, my child. I have need of you.

4

"Aine, won't you return with us?" Edan asked, hanging back when the other warriors headed back to the castle almost immediately.

"N-no," she stuttered, running a shaky hand over her forehead. *Had she really heard Epona's voice?* "I'm going to stay with Maev for a little while."

"It's not safe in the forest after dark, so you don't have much time. I'll leave the horse and cart for you," he said.

Aine nodded absently, paying little attention when he left. All of her concentration was focused internally. "Epona?" she whispered, feeling foolish.

Listen, daughter. One who needs you is near.

Aine's body trembled with excitement. The Goddess was speaking to her! Holding her breath, she listened.

A low, painful moan seemed to drift on the cool night air, mixing with the scent of death and smoke and pine. Aine turned into the breeze and followed her Goddess's urging.

The panting sounds of pain weren't hard to track. Aine was amazed that she and the warriors hadn't heard them earlier. She'd walked only a few feet into the surrounding pines when she came to the gully. What she saw at the bottom of the trench in the earth had her freezing with shock and disbelief.

The winged creature lay crumpled on the ground, its leg caught gruesomely in an iron trap so large it must have been set for the vicious brown bears that liked to lurk close to the castle.

It is your choice, daughter, whether you aid him or not.

"But he's a Fomorian!" Aine said.

Epona didn't respond, and Aine could feel that the Goddess's presence had left her. At the sound of her voice the creature's head snapped up. With eyes glassy with shock and pain he stared at her.

"Are you a goddess or a spirit?"

His voice was a surprise. It was deep and

beautiful, almost musical in quality. And he sounded frightened.

"I'm neither," she replied. Then she pressed her lips together, thinking that it was madness that she was speaking to him, to *it*, instead of running screaming for the warriors.

"You look like a goddess," he said.

Then he smiled and even as Aine cringed back from his fangs that glistened in the dying light, she felt drawn to the unexpected gentleness in his eyes that so perfectly matched his expressive voice.

"You're a Fomorian," Aine said, as if to remind herself.

"And you're a goddess."

"Fomorians are demons!" she blurted. "What could you know about goddesses?"

"Some of us know of Epona. Some of us…" he trailed off, sucking in his breath as a spasm of pain shot through him.

Responding automatically to his pain, Aine was half-way down the gully before she realized she'd moved. The Fomorian had closed his eyes to ride out the wave of agony. His forehead was pressed to the ground and he was breathing in shallow, panting gasps. *Just like any man in terrible pain*, she thought.

Then his wings, which had been tucked along his back rustled in restless agitation and she stumbled to a halt mere feet from him, eyes riveted on those dark pinions. They weren't made of feathers, but seemed to be a soft membrane, lighter on bottom than top. They were huge, and they proved what he was—what he must be. A demon.

This was what killed Maev! The knowledge rushed through her mind and she stumbled back.

"My name is Tegan."

At the sound of his voice she stopped. His eyes were open again, and even though his face was shadowed by pain he tried to smile at her once more.

"What is your name, goddess?"

"Don't call me that," she snapped.

"I meant no disrespect. I only—"

"You killed Maev!" she interrupted.

5

"I have killed no one," he insisted. Making an involuntary beseeching gesture, his arm lifted and Aine saw the short sword sheathed at his waist.

"I don't believe you. How could I? You're a Fomorian. A demon. My enemy." Aine's stomach knotted as she looked frantically around. "Where are the rest of your people?"

"It's only me. I shouldn't be here. I shouldn't have sneaked through, but I wanted to see it."

"It?"

"Partholon," Tegan spoke the word like a prayer.

"But there are more of you?"

"Of course. In the Wastelands."

Aine started backing away again. "I have to warn the Guardian Warriors. Your people have to be stopped."

"But it's only me who is here," he said.

"No...you killed Maev." Then the Huntress's words lifted from her memory. *The warriors know! They all know.* What was happening? How could the Guardian Warriors know about the Fomorians? Then all of Partholon should know. Maev was dying. She'd been almost incoherent. Or things had been happening so quickly maybe Aine had misunderstood. Shaking her head she spoke more to herself than the fallen demon, "It doesn't matter. I have to tell them."

"Please don't leave me." Even though she was well beyond his touch, he reached out for her and then moaned, crumpling to the ground again.

It is your choice, daughter, whether you aid him or not. As if battling against Maev's warning, Epona's voice filled her mind. The Goddess had led her to this creature. Surely she had brought her to him so that Aine would return to the castle and tell the men. But then why had Epona said that there was one near who needed her? When she'd followed the moans Aine had had no doubt that she was supposed to help whoever had been injured.

All right. Couldn't she do both? She could dress his

wounds and then go to the castle and warn them that Fomorians were near. Aine glanced down at Tegan's trapped leg. He might be injured so badly that he'd still be here when she brought the warriors back. Was there rope in the cart? Perhaps she could tie him up.

She drew a deep breath and looked from his wound to his eyes. "How do I know you won't try to kill me if I help you?"

"I'm not a killer," was his instant response.

"You're a demon," she said.

He frowned. "Is it because I have wings that you keep calling me that?"

"It's because your people betrayed the good faith of my people and tried to slaughter them that I call you that."

"How long ago?" he asked quietly.

"What?"

"How long ago was the war between our people?"

Aine moved her shoulders restlessly. "It's talked about in our legends. The bards sing songs about how demonic and hideous your people are." She closed her mouth, then all too aware that even though the winged man trapped so painfully on the ground in front of her might be a demon, he definitely wasn't hideous.

"Three hundred and twenty-five full passes of all four

seasons have gone by since my people fought yours," he said. Tegan paused to grimace in pain. After several short, panting breaths he continued. "So it is for something that happened between people long dead that you hate me."

"I don't hate you," Aine said automatically.

"Then help me. Please, goddess," he said.

6

"Stop calling me a goddess," Aine said, beginning to walk slowly towards him.

"I don't know what else to call you," Tegan said.

"Aine. I'm a Healer," she said briskly, kneeling beside his bloody leg.

His sudden laugh surprised her. What especially surprised her was that the infectious sound of it caught her attention more than a second glimpse of his fangs.

"A Healer! And I believed all luck had deserted me."

She frowned at him, thinking that luck was certainly a relative thing, and then fell into her normal pattern of distracting her patient through conversation. "How did this happen?"

"I was foolish." He paused sucking in his breath as she began her examination. Through gritted teeth he continued. "I know better than to step into a gully filled with leaves. My attention was elsewhere and I made a mistake."

"Your attention was on what?" Aine was intrigued by Tegan's physiology. His leg appeared human, but it ended in a taloned foot that reminded her of the old stories she'd read about Partholon's long extinct dragons.

"My attention was on this." Tegan gestured weakly at the pine forest surrounding them. "It's so green and alive. Everything here is so much more beautiful than the Wastelands." His eyes met hers. "Everything…"

Clearing her throat, she broke eye contact with him and continued her assessment. The trap had closed just above his left ankle. There was a lot of blood on it and in the leaves, but the bleeding appeared to have stopped. The odd-looking foot was already swelling, though, and his skin… she glanced up his body. His skin was paler than a human man's, but it seemed to glow faintly, as if it had been lit from within by a moon-colored light. His body was very man-like. He was tall and muscular and well-formed. His hair was so silver blonde that it reminded her of the moon, too. His eyes were slightly slanted and an unusual light amber color. He was, she

realized, exotic and odd-looking, but not an unattract-
ive man. Aine shook herself mentally. *Men* didn't have
down-lined wings that tucked against their bodies.

"I need to open this trap, but I'm worried about the
bleeding that might happen once your leg is free."

He nodded. "I understand."

"I need something to…" she paused, considering.
"The leather tie that holds your hair. I need it."

Tegan started to reach back, but the movement made
him stiffen with pain.

"I'll get it." Businesslike, Aine moved to his head.
Forcing herself not to hesitate, she untied the thong. His
silver hair was long and felt like silk against her fingers.
She could see that his ears were surprisingly small for
such a large being, and slightly pointed, as if the fairy
people had touched him there.

*By the Goddess! Fairy people? This creature is a
demon, not a harmless sprite.*

She moved back to his leg, glancing up but not meeting his eyes. "I'm going to tie a tourniquet above the
wound, but hopefully you haven't severed a major blood
vessel."

"It can't hurt much more than it does now." Tegan
tried to smile again, but only succeeded in a small
grimace.

"You're wrong about that," Aine said grimly, tying the tourniquet in place. Then she did meet his gaze. "Ready?"

He dug his fingers into the ground and Aine thought she caught the flash of more talons. Then he nodded. "Ready."

Aine positioned her hands on the trap, drew a deep breath, and forced apart its fang-like jaws. Tegan screamed, but she hardly heard him. As if a dam had broken, his leg was spurting the scarlet of a severed artery.

She grabbed a small piece of wood, twisting it into the tourniquet to attempt to slow the flow, but it made little difference.

"It must be cauterized. That's the only way," Aine murmured to herself, wishing frantically that she was in her well-stocked surgery with a variety of metal irons already heated and awaiting her use. Her gaze lifted unerringly to the short sword sheathed at his waist. Aine ignored his wing, which fluttered weakly as she leaned over him and pulled the sword free. "I'll be right back."

Tegan nodded, although he didn't speak or open his eyes.

Aine ran back to the hotly burning pyre. Shielding

herself against the blaze with the edge of her cloak, she thrust the sword into the fire and then stepped back.

"Hurry…hurry…" she whispered, as if the flames could hear her.

7

Aine wrapped a piece of her cloak around the hilt of the glowing sword and pulled it free from the flaming pyre. Then she sprinted into the woods. Thankfully, Tegan wasn't far away. It was almost fully dark and Aine would have hated to have to search for him in the thickness of the forest.

Goddess, there was so much blood! Tegan was lying perfectly still in a growing pool of scarlet. She called his name, but he made no response. She dropped to her knees beside him and felt quickly with her fingers. He didn't respond to her touch. Taking a deep breath, she pressed the hot blade of the sword flat against the severed blood vessel. Tegan's body jerked in automatic response, although he didn't regain consciousness. The smell of burnt flesh was nauseating, but when she pulled the sword away the fountain of blood had dried and blackened.

Aine looked up at Tegan's face. He was so still. She might have been too late. It took so little time to lose a life-threatening amount of blood when a major vessel was severed. Then shock set it. Often that killed as easily as blood loss.

Shivering, Aine took off her cloak and covered him with it. Tegan was wearing a worn linen shirt and patched leather breeches—no coat or cloak. Did Fomorians feel the cold as humans do? She knew so little about them. Aine bent to rest her fingers against the side of his throat, feeling for the pulse that should throb there. She had to press hard before she found a slight flutter. He might be dying, and there was little more she could do to help him.

Perhaps I shouldn't have helped him at all. Epona had led her to him and given her a choice, and then the goddess had left. Had this all been a test, and had Aine's choice made her fail it?

Aine was pulling her hand from Tegan's neck when his eyes opened.

They glowed a terrible golden color. With a movement so fast that it blurred, he grabbed Aine's wrist.

She tried to twist away from him, but his other hand shot out and a vise-like grip closed behind her neck.

"Stop! Let me go!" Aine choked and struggled against him, but he was amazingly strong.

"Imposssssible…"

His deep, musical voice made the word a seductive hiss as he pulled her down to him. His lips touched the place where her neck sloped into shoulder before his teeth claimed her, and she shivered, only this time not from cold. His touch was a delicious poison, seeping cloyingly into her body. Then his teeth broke open her skin and she moaned. There was no pain. Only dark pleasure coursed into her body as Tegan sucked the blood from her. His lips and tongue teased her skin as his hands gentled on her, caressing where they had been bruising.

"No… oh Goddess no…" Aine whispered, even as her own arms wrapped tightly around his broad shoulder and she pressed herself more firmly against his hard body.

As Aine's vision began to gray, Tegan shifted, so that he was on top of her. Her last sight was of his massive wings rippling and then spreading erect over them as if he were a mighty bird of prey.

8

Tegan came back to himself locked to Aine's body, drinking her lifeblood.

"No!" he cried, releasing her instantly and scrambling back. The pain in his leg jolted through him, but he gave it little notice. How much had he taken from her?

In control again, he dragged himself to her, touching her face and neck, calling her name. "Aine! Aine you must awaken."

But he knew she wouldn't. She couldn't. He'd almost drained her. Already the healthy flush had faded from her cheeks. He could feel her heartbeat getting weaker by the moment.

"You can't die. I can't bear it if I killed you."

Later he told himself he'd had no choice. That wasn't

the entire truth. Yes, what he did next he'd had to do to save her. But he'd only had to save her because he hadn't sent her away or warned her about him. He'd foolishly thought he could control the urge to taste her. Instead, he had been wounded too deeply and the instinct to take that which would heal him had been too great. Tegan had known it, even if he hadn't admitted it to himself. Or to her.

Tegan searched around in the leaves until he found his short sword. Then he ripped his shirt and with one quick slash, opened the skin over his left breast. Gently, he lifted Aine's unresisting body and pressed her slack lips to the bleeding cut.

"Drink, Aine. Save yourself."

At first blood trickled from her mouth, but as some of it washed down her throat, Aine swallowed. The change within her was instantaneous. Her eyes remained closed, but her arms lifted, encircling his torso so that she could press her lips more firmly against him.

Tegan groaned in pleasure as her arms brushed the sensitive underside of his pulsing wings, and her tongue flicked across his skin. He'd known that the exchange of blood was an intensely erotic experience, something shared only by a mated couple because of the side effects of such intimacy, but he had no mate, nor had he ever expected to. As Aine drank from him, Tegan thought how inaccurate the dispassionate descriptions the elders had given for bloodlust had been.

Then Aine's eyes opened. With a terrible cry she lurched away from him. She was scrubbing the sleeve of her dress back and forth across her mouth, her eyes wide with disgust and horror.

"Aine, wait. Let me explain." He spoke softly, as if she was a frightened fawn.

"There's nothing to explain." She got shakily to her feet. He made no move to stop her as she grabbed the sword from where he'd dropped it, holding it defensively in front of her, and backing away from him. "I tried to help you. You tried to kill me. That's obvious."

"I'm sorry. I thought I could control myself, but I was dying."

"So you tried to kill me to save yourself?"

"It's true that I needed your blood to save myself, but I would never have killed you." He passed a hand over his face. "That's why you had to drink from me. You saved me, little Healer, and in return I restored you."

"Restored me? You used me!" Aine whirled around and started to run up the side of the gully.

"Don't go, Aine—" Tegan tried to stand, but his leg gave way and he crumpled to the ground.

At the same instant Aine cried out and fell to the ground, too.

Deathly pale, she stared wide-eyed at him. "I feel your pain. What have you done to me?"

9

"We've shared blood," Tegan said.

"I know that, and while it's disgusting it doesn't make *this* understandable." Aine pointed to her ankle where the pain that had spiked through it was fading, but still entirely too real to have been a hysterical hallucination.

Tegan looked away from her, sighed, and then reluctantly met her gaze. "The sharing of blood is part of how my people mate. It binds us together."

"That is not possible."

"Listen with your heart and you will know the truth."

"Listen with my heart? That's ridiculous." But even as she spoke Tegan's eyes seemed to trap her. Aine felt pulled within their amber depths. Before she realized what she was doing, she'd taken a couple steps towards him. She came to herself suddenly and stopped so abruptly it was as if she'd slammed into a glass wall. "This can't happen."

Tegan cocked his head to the side, and gave her a sad, slight smile. "Do you find me so repulsive?" He hurried on. "I thought you a goddess when I first saw you."

"You're a demon. If there's a bond between us it's an evil spell you've placed on me."

Tegan sighed, shifting uncomfortably. "I'm too tired to place a spell on you. Evil or otherwise."

Her eyes narrowed. "So you admit you worship a dark god."

Aine thought she saw something flicker in his amber eyes.

"I do not worship darkness."

"Why should I believe you? You did just try to kill me."

"I did not try to kill you. I'm sorry I drank from you uninvited, but my intention wasn't to harm you—it was to save myself."

"At any cost."

"No. Not at the cost of your life. I stopped before I..." he trailed off, unwilling to continue.

"Before you *killed me*. And then you did this to me!"

"I'm sorry," he said somberly. "But what I did can't be undone."

"What! You mean I'll always feel your pain?"

He didn't speak for a moment, and when he finally did that rich, musical tone was back in his deep voice. "It isn't only my pain you can feel, Aine."

His voice…his eyes…they drew her. Aine took another step forward. And then another.

"This bond we've forged," he said. "It's not so terrible. It's how my people mate—how they love."

The attraction Aine felt for him was raw and strong. Even lying there, wounded and battered, she could see the powerful male creature he was and be drawn to the mystery of him.

It's because I drank his blood! Aine took a step back, shutting her mind to the fact that even before he'd forced her to drink from him she'd been intrigued enough by Tegan that she'd chosen to help him.

"I've done all I can for you. Leave. Return to wherever you came from. Just hurry because as soon as I get back to the castle I'm going to send them after you."

Aine closed her mind and her heart. Resolutely, she

turned her back on him and began to retrace the short path to Maev's pyre.

She'd taken up the reins of the cart and had pointed the horse's head down the road to the castle when the first of the pains speared down her leg. Aine gritted her teeth and clucked the horse into a sluggish trot.

The next pain made her gasp. He'd fallen. She could feel it. He was trying to walk and he couldn't. Not by himself.

"You shouldn't care." Aine told herself. But care or not, she was a Healer, and the suffering of others affected her—it always had. "Epona!" She called into the night.

"Help me. What should I do? Did you lead me to him so that Partholon could be warned or so that he could be saved?"

The silence of the night was her only answer.

Aine closed her eyes. She did her best to shut out the phantom pain from Tegan. *I need to follow my instinct.* So what did her instinct tell her to do?

The answer came at once with all subtly of a rampaging wild boar. Her heart, her soul, her body, all were screaming at her to return to Tegan.

It was only her mind that called her a silly, stupid girl as she turned the cart around and urged the horse to take her back to him.

10

Tegan wasn't difficult to find. He stumbled into the clearing where Maev's pyre still smoldered when Aine pulled the carthorse, who was suddenly acting uncharacteristically skittish, to a halt. He collapsed to the grass, not bothering to look up at her.

"Were you trying to follow me?" Aine climbed from the cart and approached him warily, wishing the piercing pain in her leg would stop.

He drew several gasping breaths before he answered her. "Not following you. Just trying to get back." He did glance up then, motioning vaguely in the direction of the castle.

"By the Goddess! To Guardian Castle?"

His brow wrinkled and he gave her a look that clearly

said he thought she might be soft in the head. "Of course not. My cave is in the Trier Mountains. I've stayed clear of the castle." Then his gaze focused on the pyre and understanding widened his expressive eyes. "This is Maev. The woman you thought I killed."

"She was a centaur Huntress." Speaking slowly, Aine corrected him. Then the truth hit her. Tegan hadn't killed Maev. She felt it just as surely as she felt the pain in his leg.

"I didn't kill her," he said.

"I know." She made her decision quickly. "Get in the cart. I'll take you back to your cave."

"And then you'll bring warriors there to kill me?"

"I don't know. I don't know what I'm going to do about you," she said truthfully. "If I touch you—help you into the cart—will you bite me?"

The slight, sad smile touched his lips again. "Do you want me to?"

"No." Aine said firmly, rubbing at the bruised spot on her neck.

"You are safe from me, little Healer. I lost control before only because I was on the brink of death. Your blood strengthened me. I am in no danger of dying, so you are in no danger of me drinking from you." He paused before adding, "Unless you wish it."

"Then I'll be safe from you forever," she said under her breath as she went to him and offered her hand.

Moving slowly, Tegan let her help him to his feet. She sucked in her breath when he stood beside her. Goddess, he was tall! He loomed over her, blotting out the darkening sky. His wings were at rest, tucked neatly against his back, but he still looked like a wild, masculine bird of prey.

"You're so small," he said suddenly. "I'm afraid I'll crush you if I lean on you. Maybe you should find me a branch I could use as a crutch. Or bring the cart closer and I'll hobble to it."

They stood there staring nervously at each other while he balanced precariously on one foot. Finally, she had to stifle the urge to laugh—albeit a bit hysterically. Could he be as scared of her as she was of him?

"I'm stronger than I look," she said.

Aine moved to his injured side and put her arm around his waist. His arm went instantly over her shoulders. She led him to the cart, careful not to go too fast. His body was warm and strong, and she could feel his wings behind her like a living mantle. She hadn't noticed his scent before, but it came to her now. He smelled of the forest and sweat and man. He also smelled vaguely of blood —his and hers. Aine was disconcerted to realize that the she found the scent alluring.

"I can only take you part of the way in this." They'd managed to get him into the flat bed of the cart and she had started the horse down the castle road. "I'll have to stop before the walls are in sight or the warriors might see us."

"So you've decided not to betray me?"

Aine looked over her shoulder at him. "I'm betraying Partholon by keeping you a secret."

"No you're not. I mean no harm to Partholon. I'm not dangerous to your people."

"Just rest while you can. You'll need your strength to get yourself back to that cave."

Tegan closed his eyes and cradled his head in his arms.

He hated lying to her.

11

"I can't take you any farther. The castle is too close." Aine pulled the carthorse to a halt.

"I understand. If you can find a branch I can lean on I will be able to make it from here on my own," Tegan said.

Aine gave him a doubtful look, but hurried to the side of the dirt road, searching under the ancient pines until she found a sturdy branch. When she returned to him, Tegan was already standing beside the cart. She handed him the branch and readied herself for the pain they would share.

"You can lessen it." Meeting her questioning gaze he continued. "The pain—you don't have to feel it with such intensity. Close yourself to it, much like you would close yourself to an annoying sound." He paused, thinking, then his lips tilted up. "Like a screeching blue jay. Ignore it. Tell yourself it's not there, and soon it will fade from your consciousness. Also, it won't be so strong when we aren't together. Our nearness intensifies the bond."

Aine grinned at him. "Yes, I'll think of you as an annoying bird."

"Not *me*. The pain in my leg." He touched her cheek. "You should smile more."

She should have pulled away from him, but his hand was warm and it felt so right against her skin. Her body liked his nearness and she found it difficult not to lean into him.

"Thank you for saving my life," Tegan said.

"You're welcome," she managed.

"I shouldn't ask anything more of you, but I must. Give me a chance to prove that I mean you no harm. Let me earn your trust."

"I don't know how you could do that."

He framed her face with both of his hands. "You know I didn't kill your centaur friend, don't you?"

"Yes."

"I can earn your trust in the same way. Our bond will strengthen and you will be able to tell beyond any doubt if I lie or if I tell the truth in all things."

"I don't—" Aine began but his thumb pressing gently against her lips stopped her words.

"I am alone in Partholon. No other Fomorians are with me. Listen with your heart. Do you believe me?" Aine stared up into his eyes. It was full dark by then, but Tegan seemed to be illuminated with a light of his own. She could see into him and she knew that he wasn't lying to her. He was truly alone in Partholon.

"I believe you."

He let loose his breath in a rush of relief. Impulsively, he pulled her into his arms. "Thank you, my little healer."

Just for a moment Aine let him hold her. It felt good to be in his arms—too good. Clearing her throat, she began disentangling herself. He let her go, but only to an arm's length.

"Say you will come to me tomorrow."

"I don't know if I can."

"You must. My leg will need your care. I have no herbs or potions for healing in my cave."

Aine frowned, looking down at his offending leg. It was torn, swollen, and blackened from the cauterization. It was a miracle that he was standing at all. A man would have been completely disabled by such an injury. Clearly, Tegan was stronger than a man, but would he be able to recover if it festered? Or would he suffer and die slowly, with Aine feeling every bit of it?

"How do I find you?"

His smile was so joyous that Aine hardly noticed the sharpness of his fangs. "I could find you anywhere, but it would be easiest for me if you would walk to the west, as near the mountains as you can and think of me."

"On the Wastelands side or the Partholon side of the mountains?"

Tegan's expression sobered. "Never on the Wastelands side. It's too dangerous. The weather changes instantly. Instead of sweet deer and fat sheep there are wild boar and mountain lynx."

Aine felt a shiver of foreboding at his warning. She sensed that there were things he wasn't telling her. It was on the Wastelands side of the pass that Maev had been killed…

"You have nothing to fear from me. I will never drink from you against your will again, and I will protect you against anything," he said.

She wanted to question him further, but his head snapped up. He scented the air.

"Men from the castle approach!"

12

"Go! Now!" Aine pulled away from him and climbed up on the cart seat. "I'll meet the warriors and keep them away from here."

"Tomorrow, Aine. Come to me tomorrow!" Tegan called after her.

Aine didn't take even a moment to look back or respond. She urged the horse into a brisk trot, trying to put as much distance as possible between herself and Tegan before the warriors found her.

Edan was the first of the warriors to reach her. He galloped up to the cart, looking irritated and sounding worried. She noticed the other four men just seemed bored and annoyed.

"Aine, why have you not returned to the castle?"

She blinked several times, putting on innocent surprise. "But I am returning to the castle."

"It has been hours, and it is fully dark," he said, now sounding more irritated than worried.

"I'm sorry. I just didn't want to leave Maev."

"Maev is dead. Nothing more can happen to her, unlike you," Edan said severely.

"I'm sorry," Aine repeated sheepishly.

One of the warriors she didn't know made a scoffing sound and told Edan, "You see? The Monro said she didn't need a watchdog."

For the rest of the way to the castle none of them spoke and Aine focused on thinking of the pain in her leg as an annoying birdand not thinking of Tegan and her strange feelings for him.

Even though she didn't consider Guardian Castle her home, Aine felt a very real sense of relief when the cart passed under the iron front gates and entered the square courtyard. It was almost not dreary with all the torches lit and the scent of food coming from the Great Hall.

"Developing a liking for the forest, Healer?"

The Monro stepped out of the shadows. Reeking of strong spirits, he blocked her way back to her chamber, which adjoined the infirmary.

Caught off guard, she wasn't sure what to say to him.

Then her promise to meet Tegan the next day jolted through her. "Yes. I, uh, I'm homesick and the forest reminds me of the Temple of the Muse. The pine trees are the same," she finished inanely.

"A word of warning—this isn't the neutered forest that surrounds the Temple of the Muse. Ask Maev." The Chieftain's words were slightly slurred and his smile was cruel. "I'm mistaken. You can't ask her. She's dead." Chuckling to himself, he walked away.

Tegan collapsed on the floor of his cave. He needed rest. He needed blood.

He needed Aine.

He closed his eyes, concentrating on slowing his breathing and controlling the ache in his leg. She could feel it, and he didn't want to cause her any more pain than he'd have to.

He hadn't planned on meeting Aine—he hadn't planned on meeting any Partholonians. He'd only wanted to escape what was coming and live out his life in peace. The loneliness had been inconsequential. The alternative was so much worse.

Until Aine—she had changed everything. He must warn her—ready her. But how? She didn't trust him. If he told her the truth now, she would turn from him.

And he couldn't bear that—not after being bonded to her.

He shook his head, amazed anew at what had happened between them. Tegan had given up the idea of ever mating years ago. Aine was a miracle—his miracle, and he wouldn't lose her. Their blood bond drew her to him, but Tegan knew that were it not for that exchange of blood she would have run from him, probably betrayed him to her people. So he must win her trust. Perhaps her love would come later.

He would have to act quickly. That time was running out was one thing of which Tegan was certain.

13

With Epona's urn clutched in her arms, Aine walked through the front gate.

"Healer, where are you off to?"

Aine sighed at the sound of Edan's all too familiar voice. Carefully, she covered the open top of the urn with an edge of her cloak. Her face a mask of polite neutrality, she turned to look up at where the warrior called down at her from the gate watch station.

"I'm going to Maev's pyre to collect some of her ashes. Her Herdsmaster will most likely send for them, and it would be respectful to keep them ready for him."

"You're probably right." He glanced up at the morning sky. "At least you have plenty of time until dusk. Be sure you're back by then. I'm hunting in Maev's place today.

I won't have time to come fetch you." Edan smiled, showing that he was no longer annoyed with her.

Aine nodded, smiled, and called "Happy hunting" to him before turning away.

Edan's newfound attention was ill-timed. Until he'd taken notice of her, no one—outside the few minor injuries and illnesses she'd dealt with—had had much to do with Aine. The men ignored her; the women made no friendly overtures towards her. Actually, the women were particularly odd. Instead of loosening up and accepting her, they seemed to do the opposite. The longer she'd been there, the less she'd seen of the women. That was yet another reason why she and Maev had become such good friends so quickly.

Maev...she felt terribly guilty about using her as an excuse. *I* will *collect her ashes* she promised herself as she stepped off the road and entered the forest. Circling around until she was out of sight of the castle, Aine left the forest and headed to the edge of the austere Trier Mountains.

Aine thought of Tegan.

It was easy to think of him. She'd done little else since leaving him. She should have been terrified of Tegan, or at least disgusted by him. Aine was neither. Of course it was because of the blood they'd exchanged that she felt like this. Aine's stomach fluttered as she remembered his lips and teeth against her skin and the erotic pull of him drinking from her. Her mind insisted she was only going to him to treat his wounds. Her body had a different agenda.

The pain in her leg had just become impossible to ignore when he spoke.

"Aine! Over here, my little Healer."

Tegan's voice led her into the rocky recesses formed at the base of the mountain range. He appeared before her like something out of a dark dream—mysterious and tantalizing. He held out a hand, beckoning her deeper into the shadows. Aine hesitated, struggling to sort through the wash of emotions that seeing him filled her with.

"I can not come out there to you. Direct sunlight is harmful to my people, and in my weakened state it would cause me much pain." His lips tilted up in that alluring half smile she remembered so well. "It would cause *us* much pain, and I would rather spare you that."

She joined him in the shadows. They stared at each other. Aine was more than a little shaken by how badly she wanted to touch him.

"Have you lost the ability to speak?" he asked softly.

"No! I—I see that your leg is better," she blurted, even though her eyes had not left his face. "I brought medicines." Aine nervously held up the urn.

Tegan didn't even glance at it. "I was afraid you wouldn't come."

"I had to."

"To heal me?"

"Yes." *And to touch you and be with you and see you smile again.*

"Come, my cave is close."

Tegan led her through a crevasse that cut deeply into the slate colored mountains. He moved slowly, heavily favoring his injury. Because of the narrowness of the path she couldn't walk beside him, but followed close behind. His wings mesmerized her. They were huge… dark. She'd never imagined anything like them. She had only brushed against them briefly last night and she wondered what it would be like to touch them on purpose—to stroke them.

She almost ran into Tegan when he stopped abruptly. He looked over his shoulder at her. She felt a breathless thrill at the passion reflected in his amber eyes.

"I can feel your desire. It's making it very difficult for me not to take you in my arms."

14

Aine forgot to breathe. "Your wings are beautiful." She watched them shiver, as if her words had been a caress. Surprised, she took an involuntary step back.

"Please don't fear me. We are bound, you and I. I would tear these wings from my body before I harmed you."

"Could you do that?" She stared at his wings. "They seem so much a part of you."

"To my people wings are the seat of our soul. Destroy my wings and you will probably destroy me."

He'd given her the gift of his vulnerability and it frightened her terribly. Not for herself, but for him. What would have happened if the bear trap had closed around one of his wings and ripped it off? It made her sick just thinking about it.

"Aine, are you worried for me?"

She pulled her gaze from his wings and met his eyes. "It's just that they're so...out there. If your wings are that important you'd think they'd be better protected."

Tegan laughed. "You'd be surprised. I'm not usually this helpless." Still chuckling to himself, he continued down the narrow path.

They hadn't gone much farther when Tegan told her, "You'll have to bend down to enter the cave, but it widens soon."

She watched him crouch and then disappear into what looked to be nothing more than an ordinary niche in the side of the mountain base. She ducked and went after him. After only a few feet the entrance spilled into a large, oblong room. There was a round opening in the ceiling, but it only let in a weak, indirect light. Mostly it served as an escape for the smoke from the well-banked fire that gave soft light and ample heat. She heard falling water and saw that the rear wall was wet with a steady waterfall which ran out through a crack in the rock floor. Along another wall were strips of smoked meat interspersed with drying herbs. The cave smelled pleasantly of pine smoke and spice.

"How long have you been here?" she asked as she began to unload the urn.

Tegan was gingerly lowering himself onto a pallet of furs. "Two full passes of the seasons."

She blinked in surprise. "And no one knows?"

"Only you. I rarely go out into the Partholon forest, and was only there yesterday because winter is coming and the hunting there is better than the Wastelands side of the mountains."

Aine began examining his leg. "So there are really no other Fomorians here with you."

"You said you believed me yesterday."

"I did. I do. It's just that this is all so incredible."

He sucked in a sharp breath as she poured a cleansing solution over his wound. Aine grimaced, but didn't pause until the leg was clean and dressed. Then she sat back, breathing as heavily as Tegan. She studied him with Healer's eyes. His wound was better today, but he looked worse. There were bruised shadows under his eyes and his skin had lost much of the luster it had the previous day.

"I'll be better now that you are here."

She frowned at him. "Stop reading my mind."

"I'm reading your face, not your mind." Tegan smiled. "Sit beside me and tell me about yourself."

Aine sat, noticing that the tip of his wing was almost touching her knee. "I'm a Healer," she said, trying to keep her attention from his wing. "I grew up at Laragon Keep. The women in my family have been Healers for generations."

"A legacy of kindness and strength." Tegan covered her hand with his as if it was a completely natural thing to do. "I have been given such an amazing gift in you."

Aine was going to pull her hand away, but then she felt it. His pulse against her skin. And in that pulse she also felt the beat of his need for her.

"You want to drink from me again." Aine's voice trembled.

"I do. I will always want you."

"Your need is especially intense now because of your injury." She concentrated on him, staring into his eyes. "It would help you heal, wouldn't it?"

"Your blood has the power to heal me, body and soul."

She did pull her hand from him then, rubbing at the spot that was still warm from his touch.

"Aine, I gave you my word I would not drink from you against your will."

"What if it isn't against my will?"

15

"I want you to drink from me and be healed. Then I want you to return to your people," Aine said.

"You want…" Tegan began, trying to reason through the haze of desire her words had caused to pulse through his body. Then all of what she'd said broke past his need. "No. I won't leave you."

"You have to. It's only a matter of time before the Guardian Warriors find you. They'll kill you. They won't care that you're not a monster—a monster is all they'll see."

He touched her cheek. "Then I am not a monster to you?"

"How can you be? You're in my blood. I feel what you feel. I'd know if you were a demon, and you're not."

Aine pulled a small knife from within the urn. Without looking at Tegan she drew the blade down the inside of her forearm. Then she turned to the winged creature beside her, offering him her arm. "Drink."

"You don't know what you're doing to me." Tegan's voice was rough, but he cradled her bleeding arm gently in his hands.

"I do. I can feel it, too."

With a moan of ecstasy, Tegan leaned forward to touch his tongue to the narrow slash in her skin. At the first taste of her, his wings shivered.

"So beautiful…" Aine breathed the words. She ran her fingers along the soft down that covered the underside of them.

He gasped her name. Pressing his mouth against her arm he sucked and licked, causing pleasure to ripple through her body. She lost herself in sensation, thrilled by the power in the wings that were unfurling over her. Tegan continued to drink from her as he pulled at her clothing. Dizzy with need—both his and hers—Aine helped him, until she was naked.

Tegan took his lips from her arm. Reverently, his hands glided over her body, pausing to cup the fullness of her breasts.

"I've never known such sweet softness." He touched

his tongue to the pink tips of her nipples. As Aine moaned with pleasure he sucked the delicate buds into his mouth, gently grazing them with his teeth.

"Tegan, please." Aine's hips lifted to rub herself against the hardness sheathed in his pants.

Tegan pulled away from her so that he could look into her eyes. "I can stop now. I will if you wish it. You must know that if we do this—if we join—then we will be fully mated, and I will not, *can not* leave you."

Aine tried to think, but all she could do was feel. She felt his passion and need, along with the heat of her own desire. Then she realized that she could feel something more than raw lust. Aine could feel Tegan's kindness, and along with it she sensed a soul deep sadness born of loneliness and isolation.

"How long have youbeen alone?"

"Longer than you've been alive."

"No more," she whispered.

She felt his despair before she saw it reflected in his eyes. He pulled out of her arms and turned away from her.

"You don't see me as a demon, but that does not mean it is your wish to be mated with me."

"You misunderstand." Aine sat up, wrapping her arms around his shoulders and drawing him back to her while the tips of her fingers splayed across the inside of his wings. "I meant that you will be alone no more."

Tegan kissed her with such fierce joy that it made her cry out. He released her instantly.

"Did I harm you?" He smoothed her hair back, peering anxiously into her eyes.

"No, love. Always remember, I'm stronger than I look."

She smiled as she worked the ties of his breeches, finally pulling the throbbing heat of him free. Aine stroked him with her hands, marveling at the thick stiffness and length of him.

He moaned her name and she straddled him, slowing impaling herself. Aine closed her eyes and arched back, taking him fully within her. With a snarl, Tegan wrapped his arms around her and shifted their bodies so that he was on top of her. Aine bared her throat to him, pulling his mouth down so that he could drink from her as her hips thrust up to meet his again and again.

With wings spread erect and pulsing over them, Tegan claimed Aine as his mate and spilled his seed deep within her.

16

"Don't go," Tegan said sleepily.

Aine looked up from lacing her dress. "If I don't return the warriors will come looking for me. They may be able to track me to you."

"Then we'll find a new place—deeper in the mountains. Just don't go."

Aine stroked the downy underside of his wing. It quivered, causing Tegan to close his eyes and moan softly.

"I will come back to you." She kissed him.

"Tomorrow?"

"I'll try. Rest and finish healing. I have a plan."

He raised a brow. "A plan?"

"I'm going to tell the Lord of Guardian Castle that

I'm not happy there. They'll have to find a new Healer. It won't surprise any of them. Maev was my only friend, and now that she's gone there's really nothing for me there."

"Then you will come to live with me?" Tegan rolled a dark lock of her hair around his finger.

"Yes." She was unable to keep the sadness from her voice.

"Why does the thought of being with me sadden you?"

"My family is going to have to believe I'm dead. That's what makes me sad."

Tegan didn't speak. There was no other way. With what was coming no one would accept their love—Aine wouldn't even accept it if she knew. That was why he had to get her away from here—before what they had was destroyed by an evil he couldn't stop.

"Perhaps you and I will begin a new family."

She looked startled. "Can we?"

He smiled and shrugged. "After the miracle of you, I believe anything is possible."

Tegan thought she looked a little dazed as Aine wrapped her cloak around her shoulders. He stood up, flexing his leg, pleased at how good it felt.

"It's much better," she said.

"Because of you."

Even when they couldn't walk beside one another, Aine and Tegan made sure their bodies touched. She brushed his wing with her fingertips. He stopped often to pull her into his arms. By the time they came to the edge of the mountains, dusk was near.

"I have to hurry."

Tegan kissed her once more, long and possessively. "Come to me tomorrow."

"I'll try," she assured him.

He watched until he could see her no longer.

"Healer! Where have you been?"

The Monro's gruff voice accosted Aine as she slipped quietly inside the front gates, thinking she was well hidden in the deepening shadows of dusk.

"I went to—" Aine paused. She'd left the funeral urn in Tegan's cave! Thinking quickly, Aine glanced around them. They were alone with no Edan nearby to contradict her. If she was lucky, he'd been hunting all day and hadn't even spoken to the Chieftain. "I went to Maev's pyre and offered more prayers for her."

"You should have been here. You've been needed."

"What is it?" Aine frowned. The Monro's words weren't slurring, but he smelled like a pub. How could the Chieftain of a Clan, and Lord of Guardian Castle be a drunk?

"The warrior Edan was wounded while he was hunting. It was that same Goddess-be-damned boar."

"Edan! Is he in the infirmary?" Monro's drunkenness forgotten, Aine began hurrying through the castle grounds.

"No. We thought it best not to move him. His spine may be broken. You'll have to go to him. He's not far outside the rear gate."

"Oh, Goddess! I'll need my surgical box and a board to brace his back."

"Those things already await you."

Aine jogged beside the Chieftain down the path that emptied into the Wastelands side of the pass, feeling a terrible sinking in her stomach. The air was thick, oppressive. This was too much like what had happened to Maev. Then she noticed that Monro was wheezing and dropping behind her. He stumbled and almost fell. Aine paused, but he brushed off her aid.

"Go on." He motioned feebly down the path. "Take the first right hand fork. Edan and the rest of them are waiting. I'll catch up."

Aine nodded and jogged away from him. *Pathetic*.

Before I join Tegan I'll get a message to the Muse.
Guardian Castle needs a change in leadership.

When she came to the fork in the road, she sprinted to the right, finding her second wind. In the thickening darkness she almost fell over Edan. He was lying in the middle of the path—alone. He had been disemboweled and his throat had been ripped out.

17

Aine sank to her knees beside Edan. She didn't have to touch him to know he was dead. Her surgeon's box was sitting neatly beside the body, just as the Monro had said it would be. There was no back brace, though.

"He doesn't need it," she whispered numbly.

"Ahhhhh, there you are, Healer."

Aine looked up into the eyes of evil.

A Fomorian stood before her. Several other creatures were behind him, carrying torches. The flickering light slicked off Edan's blood, which covered the leader's hands and face. He smiled and his dark wings rustled. There was blood in his fangs.

"I have need of a Healer," the Fomorian said.

"Who are you?"

"You may call me Nuada…or master." His laughter was horrible. The creatures behind him echoed it, making the sound bounce eerily off the walls of the pass.

Aine sprang to her feet and ran. Nuada opened his wings, gliding easily to cut off her retreat. He grabbed her arms, sinking his claws into her cruelly.

"I need your services, but that does not mean that you must remain completely undamaged."

He bared his fangs at her and bent down, but he didn't complete the attack. As he got near her skin his almost colorless eyes widened. He seemed to consider, and then pushed her so that she stumbled back towards Edan's body.

"Take her to the camp, but treat her carefully. We wouldn't want our Healer broken." His laughter followed Aine as the others grabbed her and dragged her along the pass.

Aine studied the Fomorians as they traveled. She forced herself to be dispassionate and use medical logic to assess them. Physically, they were similar to Tegan. They were the same species. That was obvious. But these males were different. They looked more insectile. They were taller, thinner, and their claws were more prominent. Some of their fangs were visible even when their mouths weren't open. Their leader, Nuada, was the most grotesque of the group. He was larger and stronger than the others. That they feared him was obvious.

Her Tegan was not like these creatures. These were the beasts of nightmare stories—what she had accused him of being. Instead of rejecting her mate, she understood what it was that had driven him into lonely exile. He didn't belong with these demons any more than she did.

The Fomorian camp was laughably close to the castle at the bottom of a ravine. Maev's dying words came back to her, *The warriors know! They know!* Fomorians had killed the centaur, and the warriors of Guardian Castle knew they were here. Not Edan, though. Aine knew in her heart that he had not been corrupted. That was why they had killed him.

Nuada grabbed her arm and dragged her to a tented structure that was guarded by several Fomorians.

"Healer, I expect you to make sure they live for at least as long as it takes the young to be brought forth." He shoved her inside the tent, throwing her surgical box in after her.

Aine blinked, trying to accustom her eyes to the sudden brightness. The opulently decorated tent was lit by hundreds of candles. Women lounged on cushions, sipping wine and eating pastries. She recognized several of them as women who had ignored her when she had first arrived at Guardian Castle.

They were all pregnant.

"Oh, good. You're finally here." A blonde with a bulging abdomen motioned regally at Aine. "I'm having some discomfort and the wine is not dulling it. I need you to give me something to relieve the pain."

Aine stared at her, swallowing down her fear and revulsion. Those creatures out there were not Tegan, just as she was not these women. "You're pregnant with a Fomorian's child."

"Of course."

"Why?" Aine said, not hiding her disgust.

The blonde's eyes went cold and mean. "That is not your concern. You're here for us."

"We're bringing a new species into this world," a plump redhead said dreamily.

"An army that will worship us and our beautiful, three-faced god."

Aine felt sick. They worshipped evil; they reveled in it.

"Quiet! She's only here to stop our pain." The blonde gave Aine a cruel look. "Now, do you brew us something or do I call Nuada and tell him we don't need you after all?"

Aine pulled opiates from her surgical box while she concentrated her mind on one thing, over and over: *Tegan, be wary, but come to me...*

18

Tegan arrived with the next dusk.

His sword slicing through the rear of the canvas tent made a distinctive sound. He held open the flap and offered his hand to her. Aine looked at the women she'd drugged one last time before taking his hand and turning her back on them. They didn't speak until they were well beyond the Fomorian camp.

"Did you know about them?" Aine was facing him, arms wrapped around herself as if anticipating a physical blow.

"I knew my people had given in to evil. I knew they were planning an attack on Partholon. I did not know about the women."

"They're dead," Aine said in an emotionless voice.

"The women?"

"I killed them. They were all completely mad. I gave them an easy death before they could bring more demons into this world."

Tegan's head shook back and forth over and over. "You shouldn't have killed. The darkness taints you like that."

"And what should I have done?" Aine was weeping openly. "Run away? Hide?" She rounded on him, shoving hard against his chest. Tegan made no move to defend himself against her. "You're not like them! You're not a demon, but you did less than nothing. You didn't stay and fight. You let evil win."

His voice was hollow. "If I'd stayed I would have become what they are. The darkness infected them. I left because I wanted to live without darkness."

"You left and let darkness rule. What did you think would happen to Partholon if you stayed silent? What did you think would happen to us?"

"I wasn't thinking about Partholon when I exiled myself. I just wanted to be free of evil and death. I didn't expect to meet you. I didn't expect to love you."

Mocking applause sounded from the darkness. Nuada stepped out of the shadows. "What a moving speech, brother."

Tegan stepped between Nuada and Aine. "We're not brothers anymore," he said.

"We still share the same blood." Nuada's smile was feral as he looked beyond Tegan to Aine. "I see more blood that I'd like to share with you."

"You'll have to kill me first."

"As you wish."

The shadows behind Nuada stirred. Aine saw at least a dozen Fomorians awaiting their master's command.

Then Tegan changed before her eyes. His wings unfurled. His fingers became talons. His eyes blazed with anger. "Run and live! I will find you." He told her in a voice magnified by power before he leaped forward to meet Nuada's attack.

Aine ran, but only until she understood no one was following her. She doubled back, creeping quietly along the mountain paths until she heard an odd sound. It was out of place in the night, and it reminded her of something. She almost didn't identify it, but just before the screaming started she realized that it sounded much like Tegan's sword slicing through the canvas tent.

With the first scream the pain hit her, driving her to her knees.

Aine didn't know how long she'd been unconscious. She woke up in the gloaming of predawn with a single thought: find Tegan.

Her body felt heavy and off balance as she stumbled, drawn forward by a relentless invisible thread.

When she found him it was too terrible for her mind to fully comprehend. She could only stand there, immobilized by despair and loss.

They'd cut his wings from his body. That sound she'd heard had been metal slicing through the flesh of his soul.

Then Tegan moaned and the Healer in her took over. She ignored everything: the raging pain that seared through her body in tandem with his and his pleading to let him die. Aine worked methodically. She pulled him into the shadows. Calling on strength she didn't know she had, the Healer half-dragged, half-carried Tegan to his cave. Then she went to work with his sword, trimming the ragged edges of his eviscerated wings. She used the same sword to sear the flesh that wouldn't stop bleeding. Finally, she filled Epona's funeral urn and bathed his body, mixing cool mountain water with her tears.

His eyes opened when it was all over. "You should have let me die."

"I couldn't," she said.

"He took my soul."

"No, love, he couldn't. Your soul is safe with me."

Tegan closed his eyes against the tears that streamed down his pale cheeks.

Aine did the only thing left to her. She prayed.

19

Aine used Epona's urn to pour a libation circle around her. Then she knelt in the middle of the cave under the round opening that showed a night sky filled with the brilliance of a full moon. The Healer spread her arms wide and lifted her face to the heavens.

"Gracious Goddess Epona, please hear me. I have nowhere left to go. No one else to turn to. Forgive me. I killed those women. I love a Fomorian and I'm too weak to leave him, even after I've seen what he could become. Goddess, I've felt you throughout my life, even before I heard your voice. I used to believe I only knew your presence when I healed someone, but I've come to understand that you were always closest to me when

I failed. I don't deserve your love or your help, but I'm asking for both. And I'm asking for Tegan, too."

The sky above Aine shifted. The stars that littered the night began to whirl wildly, funneling into a shimmering cone that rained light through the roof of the cave. Aine heard Tegan's gasp of shock as the figure of a woman materialized in the air above them.

Aine's eyes stung with the effort it took to gaze upon the Goddess. With a gentle smile, Epona passed a hand before her visage, and her divinity dimmed and became bearable. Aine felt the raging pain as Tegan struggled to lift himself so that he could bow before Epona. She started to move to help him, but the Goddess was there before her.

Epona knelt. She took Tegan's face between her hands and kissed him gently on the forehead. The phantom pain in Aine's back instantly cooled.

"My Goddess!" Tegan cried. His body was trembling, but his eyes were no longer haunted with pain and grief. "Forgive me for not being stronger."

"Tegan, my son, your strength is a deep, quiet well that rests within you. It nourishes without drowning your judgment. And when it's needed, you pour and pour from it. I am well pleased by you."

Then Epona turned to Aine. The healer began to kneel, but the Goddess's hand on her arm stayed her.

"Not long ago I gave you a choice, my daughter," the Goddess said. "As with the mate of your soul, I am well pleased by you."

"I killed those women." Aine's voice was choked.

"You did. Again, you had a difficult decision to make and you followed your heart. Would it help you to know that the people of Guardian Castle made their own decisions, and because they invited darkness into their midst they have been corrupted by evil? For many years to come they will pay the consequences of their choices. The ones whose spirits you set free are lucky. Their death was painless. Others will not be."

"So you forgive me for it?"

"You had my forgiveness before you asked it." The Goddess smiled. "Your life has been short, but you have a strong spirit and you are ready for the journey ahead of you. So Aine, Healer and daughter, I give you one last choice."

Epona took Aine's hand and led her over to where Tegan sat looking strong and whole again, though he no longer had his beautiful expanse of wings. The Goddess joined their hands before she continued.

"I give you the choice of your destiny. You may warn

Partholon of the coming Fomorians or you may escape from this world into one where technology rules and the beings here are merely stories of myth and magic. If you stay in Partholon you will not be safe and your love will not be accepted. If you escape to the world of technology, you will begin new lives and grow old together. Know before you choose that I will bless your decision either way. I give all of my people free will— even my champions."

Aine met Tegan's eyes. She didn't need to ask him. Their bond told her that his choice was the same as hers. She didn't blame him for it. It was who he was in the deepest well of his soul. She should know—she held that soul safe for him.

Aine looked into her Goddess's eyes. "We choose Partholon."

20

Epona's smile was blinding in its brilliance. "Well done daughter! You have passed my final test. You've chosen the difficult task, to save my people. And because of your courage, you will actually have both worlds—and by living in the one, you can know that in time you will save the other. And you will need this. It is your destiny to keep it safe until the day Partholon has need of it." The Goddess made a graceful gesture with her hand and the funeral urn floated to Aine. Startled, the Healer reached for it, but it slipped through her hands to clang against the floor of the cave.

Chagrined, Aine hastily picked it up, horrified to see that a hairline crack had appeared in its base.

"Forgive me Goddess!" Aine cried.

Epona laughed joyously. "Little Healer, you couldn't be more perfect. I want you to remember this urn. The next time you see it you will know that the time of your destiny is near."

"I don't understand," Aine said miserably.

"You will. Just remember that this urn must return here with its likeness, and you and Tegan will be the ones to ensure that happens."

Before Aine could ask any of the many questions swarming through her mind, the Goddess placed one hand on her forehead and one on Tegan's. "Go with my eternal blessing."

Aine, Tegan, and Epona's urn disappeared.

Fifty years later. Northwest Oklahoma not far outside the town of Locus Grove.

The enormous mansion was a sprawling Victorian, as out of place in the Oklahoma countryside as it would have been on top of a slate colored mountain range. It was once beautiful, but age had cracked and crinkled it until it reminded some people of an old smoker's skin.

The ancient couple who had lived there loved it.

"Do we really have to leave this place?" The old man

asked his wife. "I hate to see all of our things auctioned off like this."

"It's better this way—easier," she said. "Besides, our job here is almost over. Look, it's already happening." She motioned for her husband to join her at the window. Together, the two watched the scene in the backyard unfold.

"My God! What the bloody hell is this?" A man with an accent cried, placing the item haphazardly back on the table.

Another man picked it up and blanched in horror as he, too, saw the hairline crack in the urn's base.

"Sir, you are correct. Please accept my apologies for this damaged merchandise. Your bill will be corrected immediately."

The old woman smiled as she watched a beautiful girl with wild red hair approach the man and speak with pretended nonchalance. "Excuse me, but what will happen to the pot now?"

"It will be re-auctioned, *as is*, of course," the man said.

The couple continued to eavesdrop on the events of the auction, but only until the redhead bought the urn and drove off their grounds with it tucked into the seat beside her.

"She did look amazingly like the Incarnate on the urn," the old man said.

"That's because she *is* the Incarnate on the urn, or at least she will be very soon."

"Hard to believe someone so—" he paused, trying to decide on the right word, "—modern is going to stop the Fomorian invasion."

The old woman laughed. "At first she's going to believe that she's divine by mistake. As if Epona makes mistakes!"

"The Goddess's ways are not always clear," he said.

"No, but they are always interesting," she said. "Shall we finish this, love?"

Instead of answering her, he approached his wife. Facing her, he took both her hands in his own. "It has been a long, full life, hasn't it, Aine?"

"It has been, just as our Goddess promised."

"Because through her will we were able to escape *and* save Partholon," Tegan said.

Not only through my will, but also through your strength and willingness to sacrifice yourselves to defeat evil. Epona's voice filled the room with ripples of magic and love. *Now, my children, it is time you came home.*

Still grasping hands, the old couple's bodies began to

shimmer, and then their crooked, wrinkled forms fell away, leaving a beautiful dark haired woman with eyes the color of a spring sky, and a tall, lean man whose wings unfurled majestically as he threw back his head and laughed with absolute joy. Tegan took Aine into his arms and kissed her passionately as they faded from the modern world to reappear in their Goddess's verdant meadows, where she welcomed them with song and laughter and love.

* * * * *

Love P.C. Cast?
There are more **Goddess of Partholon** *stories available.*

Don't miss

DIVINE BY MISTAKE
DIVINE BY CHOICE
DIVINE BY BLOOD
BRIGID'S QUEST
ELPHAME'S CHOICE

The Amazon's Curse

GENA SHOWALTER

1

Nola stood in the center of the battle tent, watching as her sisters-by-race lined up. Each shifted eagerly from one foot to the other, clutching their weapon of choice. She spotted several axes, a few spears, but mostly swords.

Mating season had officially begun.

Soon the females would break into groups, fighting each other for the right to whichever stolen slave they desired. Those slaves, eight in number, were currently chained to the far wall at the end of the spacious enclosure. Three dragon shifters, two centaurs, two male sirens and a vampire. All eight were muscled, beautiful…and all but one was grinning. The vampire.

Her vampire. Zane.

The men would be bedded this night and for several weeks to come. Then they would be freed, never to return. That was the way of the Amazons. Capture, breed and abandon. Of course the males were happy about this. All but Zane.

Zane had dark hair, equally dark eyes and the fiercest temper she'd ever encountered. He didn't like to be touched and had actually injured many Amazons—not an easy feat—in his quest for freedom. Finally, in an effort to tame him, they had stopped feeding him the blood he needed for strength. Now he was physically weakened, only able to lean against the wall and wait for his mistress to be declared.

However, nothing could weaken his hatred—or the promised retribution that radiated from him.

Nola had met him what seemed an eternity but had actually only been four months ago. He'd desired her, had tried to win her affections—and she'd tried to kill him. With the memory, guilt filled her. But in her defense, she hadn't known him then. Had only been concerned with her own survival. The gods had swept them to a remote island, along with several other creatures, and pitted them against each other, forcing them to fight, to watch helplessly as their friends were executed.

More than that, she'd spent her entire life hating men

and the pain they brought with them. As a young child, she'd been sold by her own mother to male after male; she'd been used, hurt, taunted...ruined. Zane's desire had frightened her, and she had lashed out.

And now, she was paying for that.

No one could see her. No one could hear her. Though she was encircled by the bright, golden light seeping through the tent's apex, no one knew she was there, that she'd been among them, month after month. The gods had cursed her with invisibility when she'd been eliminated from their impossible contest—and then chained her to this camp as surely as Zane was now chained.

The gods had seen to Zane's captivity, as well, gifting the vampire to the Amazons to use as they saw fit. And use him they would—and had. Because mating season had not begun until today, they had forced him to work their land, hauling boulder after boulder for the building of more tents. He'd had to find sticks and sharpen them into weapons. They'd even forced him to feed many of the women by hand. Of course, he'd tried to escape, so they'd resorted to starving him. That starvation caused him to weaken unbearably, rendering him useless. Lately all he'd been able to do was lie in place and curse.

"Stand before the slave you wish to claim," Kreja, the Amazon queen, commanded. She stood at the edge of her royal dais, her gaze scanning, expectant. She was a lovely woman, with pale hair and light eyes, both of which gave her the appearance of fragility. But she possessed an iron core, a vicious nature.

The warrioresses broke apart, as Nola had known they would, and crowded around the males that tempted them.

Nineteen of the thirty-two females chose Zane.

She had hoped their aversion to biting and blood would deter them. She should have known better. Strength was prized among the Amazons, and Zane had nearly won his freedom. Twice. They wanted that strength for their offspring, which was the entire point of mating season.

"Excellent," Kreja said with a grin.

Zane snarled.

That delighted the women around him, edging them to a new level of eagerness.

Nola fought a wave of anger, of helplessness. She should not have feared Zane. She should have enjoyed him while she'd had the chance. His was the first touch in the entire span of her life that had not filled her with disgust. There had been something almost…reverent in his every gentle caress. If she'd welcomed him, he might have helped purge the demons of her past. He might have saved her from herself.

Now, she would never know.

"Fight for me if you wish," he said through sharp, gritted teeth, "but know that I will slay the winner with my bare hands."

He was not a man given to boasting, Nola knew.

"So vengeful," someone twittered happily.

"So mine," another snapped.

"It is *I* who will win his seed," still another growled. "I who will give birth to his offspring."

"No one will bear my child," he roared.

He is not meant to be a slave, Nola longed to shout. He was too proud, too defiant. Traits she also possessed. Which was why she had finally risen up and slain her own mother. Which in turn was why she sometimes cried herself to sleep, wishing she could claw the images from her mind.

Scowling, Nola strode forward and reached out, hoping that, for once, her fingers would do more than ghost through as she tried to shove the Amazons aside. As always, her hand slipped through their bodies as if she were nothing more substantial than mist.

A cry of frustration escaped her.

Still, no one paid her any heed.

"Those of you who desire the vampire will now enter the arena." Kreja's hard voice silenced their arguments. Together they did as commanded, bypassing Nola, even stepping through her.

"Damn you!" she shouted. "Hear me!"

Of course, they did not.

Shoulders slumping, she closed the distance between herself and Zane and sank beside him. Like the others, he did not act as if he noticed. But she could almost— almost—feel his warmth, and goose bumps broke out over her skin.

"Lily," Kreja called with a wave of her hand.

Lily, the child-princess who would one day rule this clan, stood up from her throne atop the dais and walked to her mother's side, her little body draped in velvet robes rather than the leather straps and skirts worn by the warrioresses.

She had changed much in the past few months. No longer was this queen-in-training giddy and innocent. Once having run from camp to prove herself worthy of her people—thereby inadvertently beginning a war between the Amazons and the dragons, a war she'd thought had caused the deaths of Nola and another Amazon—she was now solemn, determined to become a worthy leader. She'd even relinquished her right to claim Brand the dragon shifter, another of the gods' exiles, as her personal servant, and had offered him up to her people. He now sat among the other slaves.

"You will not fight to the death," Lily proclaimed in her soft voice. "But you will continue to engage each other until only one of you is left standing. It is she who will earn the right to bed the vampire."

After Nola's own experience with the gods' cruel contest, she had no desire to watch another. For Zane, however, she would watch. And she would wish.

There was only a slight pause before Kreja said, "You may begin."

Immediately the women leapt into action. Metal clanged against metal, grunts abounded, and sand was flung in every direction. Bodies were collapsing, cries of pain echoing, as one pink-haired female savagely worked her way through the masses.

Soon, she was the only one standing.

Nola wanted to vomit.

"And so we have a winner." Kreja motioned to Zane with a wave of her hand. "Claim your prize, beloved. Know that we are proud of the strength and tenacity you have demonstrated today."

As the female approached, Zane trembled. In rage. Perhaps in fear.

"I won't let her have you," Nola vowed, though she knew there was nothing she could do to stop what would happen.

2

The female was going to kill him, Zane thought dazedly, dispassionately.

She'd won him, however long ago she'd fought for him—one day? Two? Weak as he was, he'd lost track of time. All he knew was that she'd tried multiple times to bed him. But she needed a hard cock for that, and he hadn't given it to her.

Denying her had delighted him.

Now two of those wretched Amazons stood around him, staring down at his naked body. If he hadn't been half-starved and teetering on the brink of total collapse, those stares would have sent him into a killing rage. He hated being looked at as much as he hated being touched.

He'd spent too many centuries as the demon queen's whore, hers to use, hers to hurt. And he'd suffered those indignities willingly, all for the love of a woman. A slave, as he was supposed to be now. Marina, that detestable queen, had promised to set his beloved free if Zane pleased her until she grew tired of him. But she'd never grown tired of him, and Cassandra, his chosen mate, had begun to hate him as a result. Yet, still he'd stayed, determined to finally win his prize.

And then Layel, the vampire king, had done the impossible and drained the demon queen, finally freeing both Zane and Cassandra, and he'd thought to earn back her love. After all, everything he had done had been for her. Only, she'd fled him. For another man. Perhaps that was for the best.

Zane was not the man he'd once been. He eschewed females and wanted no part of them. Wanted no part of sex. He shuddered at even the thought of it. The things he'd done…the things that had been done to him…sickness churned in his stomach. Had he eaten that day, he would have vomited.

But then Nola had walked into his life. Beautiful, passionate, fierce Nola. A woman who hadn't wanted him, who had rebuffed him. A woman he'd craved with every ounce of his being, despite what had been done to him. A woman the gods had taken from him. He did not know if she'd survived their island game or if the gods had set her free, but sometimes he would swear that he smelled her sweet scent, felt the gentle glide of her hands.

The first time he'd seen her, he'd thought her a gift from the gods. For why else would he have been able to endure—no, enjoy—her touch and no other's? Now, he thought that perhaps she'd been another curse. He craved her still, yet like Cassandra he could never have her. *What did I do to deserve this?*

"I'm strong," his "owner" said now, drawing his attention, "so of course he desires me. I mean, look at what I did to my competitors! Eighteen against one, yet I *owned* that arena. But he's too weak to be claimed."

"He needs blood," another said.

"Yes, but if he's given blood, he'll be able to raise his head and bite me."

Both of the females shuddered.

Did these Amazons—who abhorred the biting of flesh and the drinking of blood and who thought to rape him to steal a child from him—not realize the child of a vampire would most likely need to bite and drink blood to survive?

Would they kill the halfling if it proved to be more

vampire than Amazon? Even through the haze of weakness, rage sparked inside his chest. He would kill them first.

Perhaps they meant to feed the child as they'd fed him, he thought next. The idea mollified him somewhat.

Before his last escape attempt, they'd kept him nourished by allowing him three small cups of blood a day. Who had donated the blood, he didn't know. Didn't care. What they didn't realize was that he never took from a living source. He only took from those he'd killed. As he was too weak to hurt them, they were in no danger of being bitten. Even starved as he was.

He would be lying if he said he didn't enjoy their fear and distaste.

But all of that was moot, he knew. He would *never* leave a child of his behind. What was his, was his.

"Did you try manipulating his rod?"

"Of course. He's not my first slave, you know."

"Well, give him blood, then bind his mouth. That way, he'll be strong enough to bed but unable to nibble on you."

"Oh, excellent idea! Grab a goblet." The pink-haired woman—he hadn't cared to remember her name—palmed one of her daggers, sliced a groove in her wrist and held the wound over the offered goblet.

His mouth watered at the sight and smell of that crimson nectar; his fangs elongated.

She approached him and held the cup to his lips. Thankfully, her skin did not touch his. "Drink."

He obeyed, swallowing three precious mouthfuls. Instantly, warmth spread through him, followed on its heels by strength.

"It's working. His color is returning." The cup was removed from his mouth, and he found his gaze locked with that of his captor. She was pretty, if he cared for such things. He didn't. He only cared that she had pink hair rather than black, brown eyes rather than turquoise, and she did not smell like Nola. Like sea and storms and flowers.

There was a pause, then a purr of agreement. "He's beautiful, isn't he?"

"Don't forget he's mine," was the snapped reply.

"Well, his cock is still flaccid, so you won't be claiming him any time soon," the other Amazon lashed back.

As the blood continued to work through him, the lethargy that had plagued him all these many days dissolved, leaving energy in his muscles, a sizzle in his bones. *Escape,* he thought, a growl working its way past his throat.

Both Amazons jumped away from him with a yelp.

"Hurry! Let's bind his mouth."

"Don't touch me!" Growls intensifying, Zane jerked at the chains circling his wrists and ankles. He hissed and snapped, kicking as much as he was able as the Amazons maneuvered around him. "No touching! Do you hear me? I'll kill you."

Suddenly a golden ray of light spilled inside the tent, and he would have sworn he caught a glimpse of Nola.

"No—" He stilled, his heart slamming against his ribs.

His captor moved, reaching for his neck, blocking the vision.

"Out of my way!" he shouted, bumping his hip against hers and sending her toppling to her face. He'd imagined Nola before, there in the battle tent. This vision, he planned to enjoy as long as possible.

Sure enough, there was a shimmering outline of long black hair, a glow of turquoise eyes, as Nola tried ineffectually to tug his captor away from him. He lost his breath. *So lovely*. His shaft hardened quickly and painfully. Nola. His sweetest tormentor.

Sadly, the illusion didn't last more than a few seconds. He wanted to scream and hurt and maim. To kill and be killed. The desire came too late, though, his stunned immobility costing him. The Amazon was able to leap to her feet and easily hook a thick strap of material around his mouth.

"Finally." Sighing with satisfaction, she leaned away from him, crouching on her haunches and smiling smugly. "And just as I suspected, your rod is—" Her words halted and her smile faded as his cock withered before her eyes. "But…you were…why…"

He had only imagined Nola; he knew that, but he couldn't stop his gaze from searching for another glimpse of her. To his dismay, he saw only furs, carved furniture and weapons. Even as his captor attempted to arouse him once more, stripping for him, caressing him, he did not stop searching.

Finally, exasperated with him, the Amazon dressed and stormed from the tent, leaving him alone with his insanity.

3

As many times as Nola had been chained and used in her life, she knew the humiliation, frustration and helplessness Zane was feeling. He must want to kill Amelia, his new owner. *She* did.

Hurting another Amazon went against every instinct Nola possessed, every rule she'd ever been taught, but she would have sliced the warrioress to pieces if she'd been able to grip a blade. Zane's eyes had been so wild, his snarls desperate. And she'd been unable to aid him, had only been able to watch in horror.

"I will take his place," she shouted to the ceiling, not knowing if the gods were listening. Or if they even cared. Zane didn't deserve this. No one did. But at least she had endured servitude before. The women wouldn't rape her, of course, but they *would* work her and beat her, both of which she could survive.

Air sucked through Zane's nostrils, and his body suddenly jerked. Then he began struggling against his bonds again. Her attention whipped to him. He was staring directly at her, his dark gaze boring into her.

"Zane," she said, rushing to his side and kneeling. "Shh, now. Shh. You'll only injure your wrists and ankles further." Already he was bleeding, losing the blood he'd just been given.

He tracked her every movement.

Could he...no. Not possible. No matter how many times she'd wished otherwise, she'd remained as un-noticeable as the air he breathed. Besides, if he knew she was here, he would be fighting her as he'd fought Amelia. Perhaps even more violently. How many times, before this terrible punishment, had she rebuked his advances? Tried to hurt him? Called him vile names? All because she'd been too frightened of her feelings. *I am not worthy of being an Amazon warrioress.*

Frantic, Zane rubbed his jaw against his shoulder until the material fell away from his mouth. "Nola," he rasped. "Nola, Nola, Nola."

He *could* see her. Oh, gods. Oh, gods! Could she touch him? Her arm shook as she reached out, meaning to brush his hair from his face, but as always, her hand ghosted through him. She moaned in frustration.

He laughed, the sound full of sweet satisfaction. "I've finally slipped over the edge of sanity and I don't care." He relaxed against the blankets spread out beneath him. "My Nola, here to comfort me. As beautiful as ever."

His Nola? A shiver moved through her. Oh, if only... "You aren't imagining me, Zane. I'm truly here. I've been here since the day of your arrival."

Zane didn't seem to hear her. His gaze was too busy drinking her in. "Of course I would imagine you like this, soft and lush, but still not mine to possess."

"Listen to me. The gods cursed me, as they cursed you, only I am not to be seen, heard or felt." Until now. Why, why, *why* could she now be seen and heard but still not felt?

Finally, her words seemed to take root. His eyelids narrowed and his lips pulled tight against his teeth, revealing the tips of those deadly fangs. "How can I see you now, then?" he asked, mirroring her thoughts.

"I wish I knew," she said on a sigh. Would others be able to see her, as well?

"So. Another curse is to be heaped upon me. To see, but never to touch." He turned his head from her, as if he couldn't bear to look at her another second. *That* was the treatment she'd expected from him, but it still hurt. *You deserve it. Take it like a warrior.*

At least he no longer thought himself crazy.

"Why aren't you with Brand?" he demanded.

Brand, the dragon shape-shifter who had been cursed right alongside them. "I don't…" What? She liked Brand, but she wasn't concerned with his treatment. He had not fought his captivity like Zane. He had embraced the thought of an Amazon owner. Other than Lily, that is. Lily had been too young for him, and he'd been nothing more than a maid for her. Since she'd released him to the ownership of the other Amazons, though, he'd looked nothing but content.

But even if he had not been enjoying himself, Nola still would have chosen to watch over Zane. His strength and determination, and even his wildness, drew her.

Maybe because that wildness had never truly extended to her. Even when she'd stabbed both of his shoulders with spears, he had not attempted to hurt her. He had cried out for her, wanting to be with her.

"Why haven't you used your…gift to help you escape?" she asked, ignoring his question. Much as this man had to hate her, she wasn't ready to voice her softer feelings. Even she didn't understand her change from tormentor to tormented.

His cheeks heated in embarrassment, but still he did not face her.

He'd once used that gift on her. Had slipped inside her dreams and showed her how good it would be between them. How he would kiss and taste every inch of her body, enjoy her, help her enjoy him. "You can show the Amazons the destruction you will unleash if they fail to release you."

"The gods stripped me of the ability when they sent me here. I can no longer enter dreams. Or create nightmares. They also stripped me of my ability to transport myself to other locations with only a thought."

Damn them! "There has to be a way to free you. I wish I could leave camp and visit your king. Word has spread through Atlantis that he is wed now to my sister, Delilah. They would help you, I know it. And maybe, like you, they would be able to see and hear me. But I am bound to this camp, as surely as if I were shackled. I cannot leave its boundaries." Or perhaps she could, now that part of her curse seemed to be lifted. She wanted to check, but couldn't force herself to move away.

Zane shifted even further away from her, and his chains rattled. It was another stark reminder of their doomed circumstances. "Why would you help me?"

"Because I—" She peered down at her hands. Her

fingers were twined together and twisting the leather of her skirt. They wanted to be on Zane's body, learning his every nuance. What would make him gasp in pleasure? What would make him moan? "I owe you. I hurt you, and I'm sorry for that. Sorrier than I can ever express. I want—"

"Enough," he growled, cutting her off. "I don't want your apology. I never did. I've always wanted you… your body."

Need trembled through her. "Yes." Yes. That's what she wanted, too. "But you can't touch me. How…"

"We will figure it out. Climb on top of me."

She did, straddling his waist. His eyes closed, and he arched up. She imagined his hard shaft rubbing against her and moaned. "Zane, I—"

The entrance to the tent flapped, and Amelia strode inside. "Well, vampire. I have decided—" Her eyes widened, and she stopped. "Nola? What are you doing here?"

Nola jumped up as though burned. She wanted to scream in frustration, but held her tongue. One question had been answered, at least. Others *could* see her. "Hello, Amelia." Did she sound as breathless to the warrioress as she did to herself?

"We thought you were dead."

"You thought wrong."

Amelia's dark gaze swung to Zane, then back to Nola. "Either way, you will move away from my slave."

"Nola," Zane said, and there was a warning in his tone.

A warning of what? Nola didn't face him, but squared her shoulders and forced her expression to harden. "How is he truly your slave when you have not yet battled every female who would lay claim to him? Amelia, I challenge you for the vampire."

4

"Hurry! She'll return any moment, and she'll have others with her. Perhaps the entire army."

Zane watched as Nola tried and failed to jerk the head of his chains from the iron pole they were attached to, a pole that was anchored deep in the earth. As before, her fingers merely passed through the object.

His shock had yet to diminish. Nola was here; Nola thought to help him. After her announcement, his captor had stormed out of the tent with every intention of speaking to the Amazon queen. Nola wanted him for her own.

Earlier when she'd apologized to him, it had not been remorse thickening her voice. It had been desire. Then she'd climbed on top of him without hesitation, had moaned when he'd arched into her. He hadn't been able to feel her, but oh, just the thought of doing so was enough for him.

"How do you propose to fight her?" he demanded. "You cannot hurt her, and she cannot hurt you."

"I didn't want to fight her. I wanted time. And why are you just lying there?" She peered down at him, hands on her hips, dark hair streaming wildly around her delicate face. There was the soldier he knew. "Fight free!"

"You will come with me? If I escape?"

"If I can, yes. I want that more than anything," she added in a whisper.

Again, there was no hesitation. There was even a flicker of hope in her magnificent eyes. She truly did not hate him.

What had brought about this change in her? *Doesn't matter right now.* Everything he'd craved these many months of his captivity—Nola, freedom, a chance to be together—was now being offered to him. No longer did he feel cursed. Never had he been so blessed.

He couldn't feel her? So what. Being with her was more important.

He was suddenly fueled with a fervor he had never experienced before, not even when he'd been whoring for the demon queen, desperate to save Cassandra. He wanted this. Would have this. Just as…soon as…he broke…free. For what seemed an eternity, he pulled hard at his wrists and ankles, straining so forcefully his bones eventually gave way.

Out came both his ankles; out came both his wrists. The pain of it nearly bowled him over as he sat up, then stood to trembling legs. He didn't care. He was free at last.

"I hear them," Nola gasped. "Come on." She made to grab him, but her hand misted through his body. "Damn this!"

There was no sensation, no chill, but the knowledge that she had tried to touch him caused him to shiver rather than shudder. From the very first, it had been that way. Others he ran from. Others he abhorred. Her, he only yearned for more of. Why?

"This way." She raced to the far end of the tent. "Raise the flap."

He lumbered to her, stumbling constantly, and did as commanded. All the while, his battered body screamed in agony, black winking over his vision, stomach threatening to heave. Vampires were fast healers, but he'd been without blood too long, the few sips he'd had earlier already used up.

Outside, light poured from the crystal dome surrounding all of Atlantis, heating and stinging his now-sensitive skin and making his eyes water. This kind of reaction had only happened once before. On that cursed island of the gods. The reminder of his time there infuriated him and that fury gave him strength. Tent after tent dotted the surrounding land. Amazons were scattered throughout. Some were bent over a fire and hammering at weapons; some were hanging animal hides.

"Walk behind me," Nola said, "as if you are my slave."

She moved forward, head held high. Behind him, he could hear a murmur of voices inside his captor's tent. Amelia had returned, and she had indeed brought an army with her. Zane kicked into motion. Thankfully, no one paid them any heed—until a horn blasted. The Amazons around him straightened, a few even reaching for weapons.

"Run," Nola shouted, picking up speed. "Run."

No longer content to remain behind her, he matched her pace. A forest loomed a few yards ahead, thick trees promising cover.

"Nola!" someone shouted. "Stop!"

"Vampire," his captor screamed. "Not another step. I *will* punish you."

Zane tripped over a rock. He lurched forward, his broken ankles unable to support him. When he hit the ground, he hit hard and lost every bit of oxygen in his lungs. Grimacing, he lumbered back up. Started running again.

All the while, Nola encouraged him. "You can do it. I know you can. That's the way. Just a little farther." But when they reached the trees, she stopped and screeched. "No! No, no, no."

He, too, stopped and faced her. He tried to grab her, but as always before, encountered only air. "Come. Now."

"I can't. It's like a wall is blocking me." Frantic, she tossed a glance over her shoulder at the scowling Amazon warrioresses bearing down on them. "Go. Please. Just go."

He remained in place, the screams in his head no longer for his bodily pain. He couldn't leave this woman behind. But he couldn't stay here, broken as he was. He was no good to either of them. Damn the gods to Hades!

"Will they attempt to punish you?" he asked.

"They can't hurt me. They might be able to see me, but I'm untouchable, remember?" She smiled, but it didn't quite reach her eyes. "Now go, before they take you. They will not be as gentle with you this time."

"Nola…"

"Zane. Go. *Please*. Save yourself. You are not meant to be any woman's slave."

A muscle ticked below his eye. "I will come back for you. Soon as I'm healed, I will come back." As he spoke, he walked backward. Only when she was blocked from his view did he spin and run.

5

Nola faced off with her sisters. They formed a menacing half-circle around her, each glaring at her.

"You freed my slave," Amelia growled, and several warrioresses booed and hissed at Nola.

She had always been something of a tribe outsider, so she wasn't surprised at the cold welcome. "He isn't yours, but yes," she said proudly. "I freed him."

A frowning Kreja stepped forward, separating herself from the masses and placing herself nose-to-nose with Nola. "I want five of my elite armed and hunting the vampire within the next five minutes."

Footsteps echoed as the warrioresses complied.

"And you," the queen continued, "you know the punishment for stealing your sister's slave?"

"Yes," Nola repeated. The punishment—a savage, wish-you-were-dead whipping. Not that they could administer it. But even if she'd been tangible, she would have risked it. Zane's freedom was worth losing the skin on her back. At the very least.

"Delilah returned and told us you lived still, but that did not stop our worry for you. And now I find you here, working against us. Why would you do such a thing?" the queen asked, sounding genuinely curious rather than enraged.

"The vampire had endured enough at the hands of the Amazons. Like us, he is a living being with feelings. He is courageous, wild as the animals in this forest and fierce beyond imagining."

And he would return for her. She trusted him.

Never before had she trusted a man, but she trusted Zane. Having watched him these past few months, she knew he was not the kind of man who made vows lightly. She knew he did not say things simply to placate his audience. Oh, yes. He would return.

What they would do when he reached her, she didn't know. She only knew that she needed to be with him. To see his face and hear his voice. She could live with any curse, as long as he was alive and well and with her.

Kreja sighed. "Wise words, but that does not change what you have done. Not only did you free a slave, you freed your *sister's* slave. For that, you will deal with Amelia in the battle arena. She will be armed. You will not. Afterward, if you survive, you will be whipped, as is our custom."

The queen reached out—and wrapped her fingers around Nola's suddenly solid forearm, dragging her toward the arena, Amelia close on her heels. Nola gasped in shock. *What...why...how was it possible?*

"I will not go easy on you," Amelia snarled at her.

They can touch me. Which means they can *hurt me,* Nola realized, dread sweeping through her.

Would she be alive when Zane returned?

Zane reached the vampire stronghold and collapsed at its gates. His strength—gone. His wounds—unhealed. Followed as he'd been, he wouldn't have been able to hunt for food. Broken as he was, he'd been unable to capture a single animal and feed himself.

Thankfully the guards recognized him. He was hefted over a shoulder and carted inside the palace. The touch disturbed him, but he didn't fight it. He was in too much of a hurry and knew this was the best way. By the time they reached his personal chamber, there was a

buzz of activity, his name being whispered from everyone's lips.

"Blood," he rasped as the guard lay him down on the
bed.

That guard tilted his head, offering his own neck.

Zane shook his head and closed his eyes. "Glass."
He would not take from a living source. Still couldn't
stomach the thought—unless that living source was Nola.
Once, when he'd ensured she would welcome him by
invading her dreams, he had tasted her. The sweetness
of her blood…the decadence of her moans…and he'd
reveled in every nuance of her. He would not overshadow
that precious memory by taking from someone else,
even in his desperation.

How did she affect him this way?

Perhaps he did not mind her hands on him because
he saw himself in her eyes. Saw vulnerability and pain,
fear and yearning. Perhaps they shared a similar past;
she'd alluded to such a thing once before, when they'd
been pitted against each other on the island. That meant
someone had hurt her at some point in her life. Hurt
her deeply and unequivocally. Zane wanted to destroy
that someone, bit by bit.

Warm hands settled on his shoulders and
shook him.

His eyelids fluttered open, a growl in his throat. When he saw that Layel loomed above him, glass in hand, he forced himself to relax against the feathered mattress. "My king, I—"

"No talking just yet. Drink," Layel said, placing the glass to his lips. Tall and leanly muscled, with white hair and blue eyes, he was an eerily beautiful sight that reminded Zane of both his rescue from the demon queen and the horrors he'd endured at the hands of the gods. "Drink."

Zane opened his mouth, and the sweet nectar of life poured down his throat. He swallowed greedily. Once again, warmth spread through him. Warmth and strength and determination.

He had not lied to Nola. He was going back for her. He would conquer that damn camp and everyone inside it. *Nola will not like that. Those women are her sisters.*

Well, they damn well should not have tried to enslave him, he thought darkly. But he knew deep down that he wouldn't hurt them. Not really. For Nola, he would simply send them on their way, claiming the camp as his own and remaining there until she could leave.

"Good now?" Layel asked.

"More," he said when the supply ran out. He'd need every ounce of his strength to conquer the Amazons.

Layel cut his wrist, filled the glass with his own life force, and offered it up. This time, Zane was able to hold the glass on his own. He drained every drop. When he finished, he licked his lips and faced the king.

"I am ready to talk," he said. "You escaped the gods and their island." He grunted as his wrists and ankles popped back into place. "Did you win their game?"

The king's lips slowly lifted in a grin. "Delilah did. She saved us both. We have been searching for you since the moment of our return, but the Amazons hid you well."

"Have you news of my sister?" a female voice asked.

Zane looked past his king and saw Delilah standing in the doorway. She was petite in appearance, but as fierce as Nola on a battlefield. Her blue hair was falling around her shoulders, and worry was etched in the violet depths of her eyes.

"She is alive," he told her, and she expelled a relieved breath. "And she is mine."

"And does she agree with that statement?" Delilah's head tilted to the side as she rubbed at her slightly rounded belly.

Slightly rounded. A baby? Layel was to become a father? An ache bloomed in Zane's chest. He'd wanted children with Cassandra. Had dreamed of them. Yet that, too, had been denied him. Until…now?

With Nola…*You cannot truly touch her, you fool. That dream is still dead.* He couldn't make himself care, however. As long as he had Nola, nothing else mattered.

"Well?" Delilah insisted.

Did Nola wish to belong to him? she'd asked. He thought so, yes. She had

helped him. She had even wanted to go with him. But she was also a warrior to her core, an *Amazon* warrior at that, and they only tolerated men during mating season. He wanted far more than that. No matter the circumstances. He wanted what Layel and Delilah clearly had.

"We will see," Zane said, kicking his legs over the bed.

"You only just returned," Layel said. "Where are you going?"

"To get my woman." This one, he wouldn't let get away.

6

Grunts, groans and the clang of metal against metal roused Nola from her troubled sleep. She wanted to rise, to see what was happening, but could not force her body into action. Her back was a mass of agony, the skin flayed completely. The rest of her, well, it had not fared much better during her battle with Amelia. Nola had won, her determination stronger than any weapon, but she had not emerged unscathed. There were deep sword slices all down her arms, stomach and legs.

She lay on her bed, her stomach pressed into soft blankets. Alone, always alone. No one was allowed to help her. Not in any way. Amazons healed as slowly as humans, so she knew she would suffer like this for many weeks to come.

Outside, a scream echoed. Her muscles were heavy as stones, and she didn't have the strength to drag herself upright. Or gather food. Not that she even had the strength to eat. She wanted to help her sisters, though. Despite what had been done to them, she loved them.

"You will die for this, vampires!" someone shouted.

"Not by your hand," she heard a male voice say. The vampire king?

Despite her pain, Nola grinned. Relaxed. Zane was here.

For hours, the battle continued to rage. Nola didn't want her sisters injured, but neither did she want Zane to lose, and waiting proved difficult. She chewed at her cheeks, dug her nails into her palms and broke into a sweat, which caused her back to burn as if it had been set on fire.

Finally, the tent flap rose and light flooded inside. And then he was there, standing in front of her. Her vampire. Zane. Her heart knocked against her ribs.

"Knew you'd come," she said, her voice barely audible. She hadn't screamed during her whipping, hadn't made a sound, but holding her cries inside had scraped her throat raw.

"Nola…sweet…" He approached her slowly, as if she

were a trapped animal. " What did they do to you?" There was horror in his tone. He crouched beside her, reached out and smoothed her hair from her damp forehead. Then he froze. "How is this possible? I'm touching you."

"Yes. Happened just after you'd left." Any other time, she would have been mortified for him to see her like this: broken, helpless, naked but for a sheet covering her lower half. Her relief at seeing him alive and well, however, was simply too great.

"I will destroy the gods for this. I will find a way to raid the heavens and I will—"

"No, no. This is a blessing. I've had time to think, and I believe I know what's happening. Each time I admit something about you, like the fact that you did not deserve what was done to you, and that I trust you, I've been given back a piece of my life."

His brows furrowed together, and a spark of hope entered his eyes. "Can you pass the camp boundary?"

"No. My sisters carried me there, meaning to toss me out, but that invisible wall blocked them."

Fury replaced the hope. "We didn't hurt your sisters— I knew you would hate it if we did, but now I wish I'd sliced each and every one of them to pieces. They abandoned camp or I would see to it now."

"You're here now. That's all that matters. But…how long will you be able to stay?" Her nervousness returned. His king would want him back. And the Amazons would one day come back. "You can't remain forever and I can't leave. We'll be forced to separate again and—"

"It's all right. It's all right, sweet. I'm here, and I'm not leaving without you. No matter what. You freed me. I will find a way to free you."

The burst of strength her nervousness had given her drained, and she expelled a breath. "As long as I have you, I'll be all right."

"Yes, you will." He stretched out beside her and angled his head, displaying his neck to her. The scent of him filled her nose. Dark spice and tree dew. She inhaled deeply, savoring.

"Drink," he said.

"Wh–what?" Even when they'd been trapped on that island, he had not let anyone drink from him. Not from his wrist, and certainly not from his neck.

"*Drink*. I know biting and blood are distasteful to your kind, but you will heal faster if my blood flows inside your veins."

"No, you don't understand. I don't mind drinking from you. I just don't want to disgust *you*. I know you do not like such things being done to you."

"I want to give you everything, Nola. Even this. With you and no other. I need this, so please. Please."

Please, this proud, strong man had said. How could she deny him? She cried out as she edged toward him and sank her teeth into his neck, hard as she could, cutting past skin and hitting vein. Blood instantly trickled down her throat. Once, the thought of doing this would have been distasteful to her, as he'd claimed. But this was Zane. She wanted him inside her. Any part of him that she could get. And like him, she wanted him to have everything she had to give.

"I never thought to allow someone to take from me again," he said, petting her head. "The demon queen, I was her slave for many centuries and she took from me whenever and however she desired. Her methods sickened me, but I allowed them because she had something— someone—my compliance was supposed to purchase. Did I ever tell you that?"

He was trying to distract her from her task, she suspected, as the warmth of his blood spun through her, lighting her up from the inside out. But she did not stop, because she wanted to hear more.

"When she died and I was freed, I thought to never endure such things again. You, though, I think I would allow to do anything to me. It has been that way since the first. I don't understand it, either. Your presence doesn't drown out the memories or take away my revulsion for this act with others. My...need for you simply overrides it. But why do I need you, do you think?"

Finally she pulled from him. She didn't move away, but snuggled into his waiting embrace, head cradled in the hollow of his neck. The action pained her, but only a little. She could feel the flesh weaving together on her back.

"When I was a child, my mother mated with a man and left the Amazon camp to live with him. They had no money and so they...sold me, time and time again," she said, heat spreading over her cheeks. "I know the desire to never again be touched by another. But with you..."

"Oh, sweet. I am so sorry."

That gentle tone brought tears to her eyes.

He wrapped his arm around her, careful of her injuries. "You once told me your family had destroyed you, that you had killed them for it, but I had no idea they'd done such things to you," he said.

She flattened her palm against his chest, exactly as she'd wanted to do all these months while watching him. His heart beat, fast and hard. "Maybe we remind each other of what we were like, before. Unafraid, untainted. Maybe we see the future in each other and the past ceases to matter."

He didn't reply, which disappointed her. Instead, he settled her onto the blankets and sat up, which angered her. Did he not want a future with her? Was that what his silence signified? Did he—

He traced a fingertip along her spine, and she shivered. "All healed," he said huskily. "And now, all mine."

Thank the gods. She wasn't sure what she would have done if he'd rebuffed her as she'd once done him.

"Make love to me, Zane." She'd never been with a man of her choosing. Never given herself completely. She was suddenly desperate to know what that was like. With this man. Only this man, who was surely a gift from the heavens, even amid her curse. "Please."

7

Zane flipped Nola to her back so that she was peering up at him. A gasp escaped her, but she didn't try to scramble away, even though he loomed above her, dressed in his blood-splattered battle clothes while she was naked.

Her breasts were small but firm, perfectly tipped with hard pink nipples. Her stomach was flat, her skin sun-kissed and smooth. He could see every ridge of her ribs and knew she hadn't eaten since his departure six days ago. Damn her sisters! Had she not already been through enough torment, without her tribe adding to it?

He was going to burn away the images of what they'd done to her. Burn away the memories of the men who had used her. He would replace both with thoughts of himself. He didn't care what he had to do to accomplish it.

"Have you ever experienced pleasure in the act?" he asked.

Up and down her chest rose with the force of her breathing. "No. You?"

"Long, long ago." He only prayed he remembered how to please his woman. With the demon queen, he hadn't cared to try. He'd simply endured. Never had a female's enjoyment been more important to him. "If I scare you, do something you don't like, tell me."

She nodded, nervously licked her lips. "You tell me, as well."

It was his turn to nod. Rather than suck on her nipples as he desired, he lifted himself off her, reached behind him and tugged off his shirt. He tossed it aside. His boots and pants quickly followed, leaving him as bare as she was.

Nola's gaze traveled the length of him, and fire leapt inside her turquoise eyes. "Zane…"

"Afraid?"

"No. You won't hurt me. I just wanted you to know I like what I see."

Her trust emboldened him, as did her praise. Gently

he eased atop her. Skin against skin, hardness against softness. They moaned in unison. Contact with anyone else, even his king, was hell. Contact with Nola was heaven. Her legs opened, allowing him a deep cradle.

"I want to kiss you now," he said.

Only when she whispered her consent did he lean down and press his lips against hers. Softly at first, barely even a touch. But the sweet scent of her was in his nose, her nipples hard against his chest, her thighs pliant against his, and soon he had to have more. He licked at her, and her lips eagerly parted. His tongue glided past their teeth to intertwine with hers.

He'd had her blood, but he'd never had her mouth. To his delight, this was even better. Sweeter, headier, not for living or healing or even to relieve hunger, but simply for pleasure. It was addictive, and he wondered how he'd gone without this for so long.

Tentatively, she tangled her hands in his hair. And at first, her tongue was hesitant against his. Seeking, as if she wasn't sure what to do with it. But the more he explored her mouth, the bolder she became. Soon their teeth were banging together, their bodies writhing against each other. Sweat was beading over his skin, his blood heating as though lava flowed in his veins.

"Going to…suck your…breasts now," he managed to say between pants. "Like that?"

"Yes. Yes." She, too, was panting. She, too, was sweating. Her eyes were closed and her head was thrashing from side to side.

I did that. Pride filled him as he lowered his head, fitting his lips around one tight little pearl. He laved it with attention before turning to the other one—careful, so careful to deliver pleasure without any sting.

When he kissed his way down her stomach, she quivered and gasped his name.

"Stop?" he asked. Would be difficult, but he would find a way.

"More."

Thank the gods. Never had he been more determined in his life. He would know this woman, every inch of her. Nothing would be prohibited. Body, mind…soul. Mouth watering, he licked between her legs. Wet, wild, wanton.

A memory of doing this very thing to the demon queen slipped into his mind. He'd once hated this act—until he'd tried it on Nola on that island. Oh, how he had enjoyed doing so, which had shocked him. Since then, he'd craved it—another shock. He wanted this to last forever. Nola was precious, a treasure, her cries a drug for his ears. *Do not think about the demon. She has no place in this wondrous moment.*

"Like?" *Please, please, please.*

"Mmm, yes. Before, they just ripped at my clothes and shoved their way—"

"No, no. None of that." As she'd spoken, she'd stopped writhing. Had released her death grip on his hair. "That does not belong between us. It's just you and me in this bed. You and me."

Her eyes were luminous as she nodded. "Bite me, then. Take my blood and remind me that my vampire is claiming me."

"No. No, I can't."

'Because you do not take from living beings?" she asked hesitantly.

"You, I would gladly take from. Anytime you would have me." It was the truth. "But as I told you, I know your kind abhors that, and I will never ask you to do anything you do not want to do. I will find my nourishment elsewhere."

"No!" she shouted, and it was a soldier's cry. She might appear delicate, but she truly had the soul of a warrior. "You will only ever take from me."

A possessive warrior, he realized, wanting to grin. He crawled up her body, fit his cock against her moist entrance. "I will only ever crave you, sweet. That much is true."

"I need you inside me. I need to feel you, as deep as you can go. Your shaft—and your teeth. Take all of me. Please."

Oh, that please...He'd seen the way her expression softened when he'd uttered that word. Now she thought to use it against *him*, bless her. Inch by inch, he sank inside her, careful, meticulous. Never had he exercised such exquisite care. Finally, though, he was in her to the hilt. They were joined; they were one. She surrounded him, hot and tight and wet, and it was better than he'd anticipated.

Tenderly he cupped her face. Her beautiful face. His thumbs brushed over her lips. He would care for her all the days of his life. He would ensure no one ever hurt her again. "Ready?"

"For you? Always."

He withdrew from her, almost all the way out, before sinking back in and groaning at the bliss. Her back arched, and her perfect white teeth nibbled on her bottom lip. Her head fell to the side, revealing the delicious plane of her neck. Still he did not bite her. He wouldn't. Wouldn't do that to her.

In and out he moved, in and out he savored her. He

stared into her eyes the entire time, and she stared into his. It was as if they were each other's anchor. As if seeing each other kept them here, locked in the moment, just the two of them, safe and cherished. There was nothing else, no one else, the fruition of every secret yearning he'd ever possessed.

"Bite," she commanded.

"No. You are healing."

"No, I *am* healed. Bite me. I want it. I need it. Don't deny me this. Please, don't deny me this."

"Nola—"

"Please, Zane. Please. With you, nothing seems wrong. Don't make me beg."

He could not stand the thought of this strong woman begging for anything. He bit, fangs driving into her neck. The sweetness of her taste exploded on his tongue, through his body, making his muscles quiver and his bones vibrate.

"Zane," she cried as her inner walls spasmed around his shaft. "Zane, Zane." Her hands clutched at his back, her nails digging into his muscles. "Yes, yes, yes."

"Nola!" That was all his body needed to propel into its own release. He roared, shooting inside her, filling her up with everything that he was. In that moment, his entire existence made sense. He'd been born to be this woman's mate. He'd given himself to a demon to better understand this precious woman's pain. He'd been chosen for the gods' cruel game to ensure this woman's survival.

He loved her. Would always love her.

And now, he thought, an idea springing to life, he would save her.

8

Nola cuddled against Zane's body, happier than she'd ever been in her life. She'd just made love. Truly made love. And it had been amazing. Her body had hummed with pleasure, and her mind had soared to the heavens.

Only once had she considered her past, and Zane had quickly defeated the memories, as only a strong, fierce warrior could. No one had ever made her feel as protected or as prized as this man had. She hadn't thought such feelings possible, actually.

"Zane," she said, grinning. She was buzzing with joy, drunk with it, and just might smile for the rest of her life. "Thank you."

"I did do a good job, didn't I?"

It was the first time he'd ever teased her, and she liked

it. A laugh bubbled from her; she couldn't hold it back. Soon she was laughing so hard, tears were streaming down her cheeks.

Zane's lips were twitching. "Some men would take this as a criticism of their performance."

"But as you know you did a good job…"

"I'm not one of them," he agreed.

They shared a grin.

His arms tightened around her. "You said every time you admitted something about me, you were freed from some part of your curse."

"Yes." Reminded of her plight, some of the happiness drained from her.

"Then do you have something else to admit to me?"

"Oh. Well…I—I—" Nola sat up and peered down at him. No longer did he appear so confident and joyous. His expression was blank. No, not blank. Fear was sparking in the depths of his eyes. For some reason, seeing it gave her courage. "I love you. I love you so much I ache with it." The words tumbled from her; she couldn't stop them. "I can't imagine my life without you in it. I want to make love to you every night and wake up to you every morning. And I don't want you to think I'm saying this only because I wish to lift the curse. I'm not."

"You are too honest for such a trick." He grabbed her and rolled her under him. "And just so you know, I love you, too. So much I would die without you. You are my life, my heart, my everything. Wherever you are, that's where I want to be."

She hadn't dared dream of having a man like him, or a life like they would surely lead, not even as a child. It had seemed too much to ask, too unattainable, and she had preferred to wallow in her sorrows rather than risk hope.

"The gods didn't take your ability from you," she said. "You can still create dreams. For the first time in my life, I see joy in my future."

"Oh, Nola. *You* are my joy."

With another laugh, she threw her arms around him and rolled him to *his* back. Her dark hair fell around him, forming a curtain that left only the two of them—just the way she liked it.

They made love twice more and spent several hours simply talking and getting to know each other better, before dressing and emerging from the tent. Night had fallen, but vampire warriors still patrolled the area.

Nola spotted the king and her sister in front of the fire.

There was no love lost between herself and Delilah. Nola had once tried to murder Layel, after all. She marched on, determined. Anything for Zane. Still…

"Will they…what if…"

Zane captured her hand with his own and squeezed. "They will love and welcome you or we will find somewhere else to live."

She shook her head. "I don't want you to lose everything you hold dear because of me."

"Nola," he said, stopping her and forcing her to look up at him. "*You* are all that I hold dear. Nothing else matters to me."

Tears burned her eyes. "What did I ever do to deserve you?"

"It is I who is undeserving. But you have my word, I will do everything in my power to prove myself worthy of you."

She pressed a soft kiss to his lips. "You already have."

"Nola," she heard Delilah call.

Nola turned and Zane wrapped his arms around her, keeping her in the protection of his embrace. The blue-haired warrioress was walking toward her, expression blank. Layel stayed close on her heels, a blade in his hand, as protective of his woman as Zane was of Nola.

"You are well," Delilah said.

"Yes. And you?"

"Yes." And then Delilah was there, grinning, pushing Zane aside to hug her tightly. "I've been so worried about you."

Nola glanced at Zane and he gave her a nod of encouragement. Biting her lip, Nola hugged her back.

"I thought I was going to have to burst into that tent and give Zane a stern talking to," Delilah said, pulling back and grinning. "But the moans were of pleasure rather than rebuke, so Layel was able to hold me back."

Nola's cheeks heated.

So did Zane's, she noticed. And for some reason, that eased her own embarrassment.

Layel slapped him on the back. Zane stiffened for a moment, then relaxed against Nola. "Good man," the king said with a laugh. "Doing our people proud."

"Well, shall we go home?" Delilah asked. She rubbed her belly, which Nola suddenly realized was not quite as flat as she remembered. "As protector of this little hellion, I am not the soldier I once was and prefer the comfort of my own bed."

A baby. Nola again glanced at Zane. He offered a

soft smile—one that promised they, too, would one day experience such a joy. "Congratulations, Delilah. I am so happy for you."

Delilah beamed. "Thank you."

The warrioress and her husband shared a tender smile before Layel escorted her a few feet away, to where the horses were chewing on grass. "Zane? Will you be joining us?"

"We will try," he said, but didn't explain further.

Whether the king understood or not, he merely nodded. "Back to the palace, men," he called.

Zane helped Nola atop his horse, then swooped up behind her. Nervousness skidded through her when they started forward. First Layel and Delilah disappeared beyond the trees, then the vampire troops. Soon their turn would come…soon she would know if she was still bound to the camp.

"Zane," she said, unable to keep the tremor from her voice.

He didn't say a word, just urged the horse into a quicker pace. And then they were past the trees, just like everyone else. They were in the forest, heading away from their captivity.

"We did it! We're free!"

"As I knew we would be." He kissed the top of her

head. "The gods are not the cruel monsters I imagined. How can they be, when they paired us together?"

Thank you, she mouthed to the top of the dome. Not once did she look back. There was too much to look forward to. "I love you, Zane."

"And I love you. It will be my pleasure to prove it to you, over and over again."

"Even when mating season ends?" she teased.

He squeezed her tight. "I have a feeling our mating season will last for eternity, sweet."

* * * * *

Gena Showalter's **Atlantis** *novels are available now.*

Look for

HEART OF THE DRAGON
JEWEL OF ATLANTIS
THE NYMPH KING
THE VAMPIRE'S BRIDE

for more outrageously sexy adventures!

Voodoo

MAGGIE SHAYNE

1

"Do you believe what that tour guide said about this hotel?"

"About the complimentary continental breakfast?" Tessa asked smiling, knowing full well that wasn't what her sister meant at all. "I'd believe just about anything a man who looked that good said to me, to be honest. God, what he did for those black boots…"

"I meant about this hotel being haunted? There really is a chill in here. Can't you feel it?" Tricia rubbed her outer arms, looking cautiously around their room. It was an incredible room in a small, three-story building in the French Quarter. It included an antique fireplace with scrolled hardwood mantel that must have been two centuries old, elegant hand-tooled woodwork, and tall narrow windows. French doors opened onto a balcony with wrought iron filigree railings and wicker furniture. "There is a chill. Don't you feel it?"

"I think you took that Haunted Tour a little bit too seriously. And if you're feeling a chill, it's because you just stepped out of air the approximate temperature and consistency of boiling pea soup, and into one of the few rooms in New Orleans that comes with AC."

Tricia shook herself. "AC and an antique oil lamp," she said looking at the lamp on the mantel. "But, no, that's not it."

"Honey, does this place really look like it was once a whorehouse? Hmm? Or that it burned in a horrible fire, trapping some of the women inside?" Tessa parted the curtains, peering down into the narrow streets below, where people walked around drinking beer from plastic glasses and wearing Mardi Gras beads even at this ungodly hour. "They could have jumped from here and barely bruised themselves, and we're on the top floor."

"So were they, according to the tour guide. They were supposedly trapped."

"I think the tour guide was just giving us a little New Orleans scare to spice up our visit." She wiggled her eyebrows. "Though if he really wanted to spice up my visit, I could think of better ways."

Tricia laughed, grabbing a pillow from the red velvet settee and throwing it at her sister. "Okay, fine, I'm overreacting," she said. "Maybe the cemeteries, the Voodoo Museum, and the Haunted Tour were a bit much all in one day. I'm gonna take a cool shower and go to bed."

"I'm next. Gosh, it's three a.m. Time flies when you're doing Bourbon Street, huh?" Her sister nodded on her way into the bathroom. But once the door was closed, Tessa stopped smiling, and looked around the beautiful room. Something was off. Something…she couldn't put her finger on. And unlike her sister, she did not have a tendency to let her imagination run away with her.

She took the camera from around her neck, and set it on the bedside stand. Then she wandered to the window again, parted the curtain to stare down at the street.

He was standing there. His long black hair was pulled into a ponytail, and his moustache connected to the closely cropped black beard. Trimmed, neat. He was still completely in character, just as he had been when he'd walked their group through the French Quarter on that guided tour. He wore a long black coat with a tab collar, and his tight-fitting pants were tucked into tall black boots that whispered naughty suggestions into her mind.

He was alone. Just walking along the dark street. And as she watched, he stopped, paused just a moment, then turned to look right at her. His eyes burned into hers, made her painfully aware of just how long she'd been without a man's touch. Then he smiled, very slightly, as if he could read exactly what she was thinking.

She backed away from the window, letting the curtain fall, pressing a hand to her chest to still the hungry beat of her heart. Then, slowly, cautiously, she looked out again.

But he was gone.

2

Tessa woke with a start. All night she'd been dreaming, but from the moment she opened her eyes she couldn't remember what she had dreamed about. Something intense. Something that left her skin damp and her heart palpitating. She took a second to ground herself back in the firm, solid world of reality, and finally slid out of bed and slipped into the bathroom. She ducked into the shower to start the day as she would inevitably end it—wet. It was perpetually hot and wet here in July. But already she felt as if she were getting used to it.

When she came out of the bathroom she was dressed and ready for a full day of playing tourist. But as she glanced at her sister still in bed, she frowned. "Hey, sleepyhead, wake up. Daylight's burning."

Tricia lowered the covers enough to squint at her sister. "Would you be totally bummed if I begged off this morning?"

"Are you sick?" Tessa went to the bed, pressed her palm to her sister's forehead.

"No, just drained. I'll just lie here and sleep till noon, then I'll be good to go. Promise."

"You sure you don't mind staying here alone?"

"Not during the day," she said. "Go on, go have beignets or something. Come back for me at lunchtime."

"Okay, if you insist." She wasn't worried about Tricia—her sister had never been a morning person. Tessa grabbed her straw hat and matching bag, her sunglasses, and her camera, and headed out. The first thing she did when she got far enough from the hotel, was turn back to face it to take a photo of it, which she couldn't believe she hadn't thought to do before now. But when she depressed the shutter, nothing happened. Frowning, she turned the camera toward her, looking at it. Every shot had been used up. "Well the hell? I could have sworn.…" Then she shrugged, and headed into the small souvenir shop down the block. She dropped her film off there for two-hour developing, picked up a couple of fresh new rolls at tourist prices, and went on her way again.

It was nine a.m. and already well above 90 degrees. Sweat beaded, but didn't evaporate. There was no such thing as a breeze on the streets. Only a few tourists were out and about this early. The horse-drawn carriages hadn't even begun carrying groups of them around the Quarter yet, and most of the shops were just opening for business.

She walked. She loved to walk. She walked all the way from Rue Royale to Jackson Square as the sun beat down on her, and her clothes and skin grew damp. Café du Monde was open, and already many of the tables were filled. It was covered, for shade, but the place had no sides. A lone musician, a man in a white suit with dark skin, was setting up outside it, unpacking his saxophone lovingly from its case, setting up a display of his own CDs and tapes for sale. She chose the table closest to him, so she wouldn't miss a thing, dropping a bill into the saxophone case as she passed.

"Well, thank you, pretty lady. Can I play something special for you this beautiful mornin'?"

"Something heavy and mellow," she said. "Like the air here."

He smiled as if understanding, put the horn to his lips, and began to play. Tessa ordered beignets and coffee, leaning back in her seat and letting the sweet music wash over her. Until something tingled on the nape of her neck, and she sat up again, turning and looking... and she saw him.

The tour guide.

3

The mysterious tour guide stood outside a small gift shop staring at her. She stared back for a long moment, her body heating, melting, aching in a way that was completely foreign to her. Then he broke eye contact to pick up a book from a rack that stood outside the gift shop. He flipped through it, then put it back again, very carefully, very deliberately. Again, he looked at her, his eyes burning and intense, as if he were trying to tell her something.

A large group of tourists passed between them then, blocking him from her view, and when they cleared, he was gone.

Tessa left her table to run across the street to where he'd been standing. She looked up and down, but he was nowhere to be seen. And why was she so hoping to see him anyway? What was she planning to say if she did see him? How could she explain what happened to her every time she met his eyes? It was as if parts of her that had been dormant, came screaming to life. It was as if her insides melted and pooled low and deep inside her. Her skin tingled, her heart sped up, and she thought about things she never thought about.

She supposed it was desire. She'd always been luke-warm to the advances of men until now, but for some reason, probably some inexplicable chemical attraction, she kept having the urge to rip her clothes off for this man she had barely met. Maybe it was the hot flavor of New Orleans bringing her inner vixen to life in her loins. Or maybe it was something about him.

It was probably, she thought, those damned sinful boots he wore.

Idly, she glanced at the rack of magazine-size tour books that stood outside the shop, trying to see which title he'd been perusing. She was certain he had picked one from the topmost slot. When she saw her own hotel on the cover of one of the books, and read the title, she felt her heart skip a beat. Haunted Inns of the French Quarter. Blinking she picked up the book, flipped through the pages, then stopped when she came upon the image of a nude woman who looked exactly like her. It was a photograph of a painting, and it was stunning. She read the caption.

"Prostitute Marie St. Claire was a favorite model of New Orleans artists for a 10-year period during the mid-1800s. The man who painted her most often was Marcus Lemieux, whose self-portrait appears on the next page," it read.

When she could tear her gaze from the nude portrayal of herself, she flipped the page, and found herself staring at the very face of the tour guide.

"Oh my God," she whispered. "My God, what can this mean?"

"You wanna buy that book, cher?" a woman asked slowly.

She had propped the shop door open and was smiling a welcome at Tessa.

"Yes. Yes, here." She handed the woman a twenty, muttered "Keep the change," and hurried back across the street to the table where the waitress had already delivered her order.

4

Tessa ate the sweet beignets, dusting herself in powdered sugar, while reading the tragic story of Marie St. Claire. The tour guide had left out a lot of details. Yes, he'd spoken of the prostitutes who had died in the fire, trapped in the third-floor rooms, unable to escape. But then he'd veered into tales of hauntings, things tourists had reported and experienced in the hotel since. He had left out many of the details. The fact that Marie St. Claire had been a model, that one local artist, Marcus Lemieux, who could have been his own twin, had painted her more often than any other. Lemieux had attempted to rescue her from the fire, and become trapped himself. He had survived, but his hands had been burned so badly that he had never painted again.

She closed the book, surprised to feel tears welling up in her eyes. Her chest hurt, and she found it hard to breathe. Leaving money on the table to pay her tab, she slid the book into her straw shoulder bag, wiped the sugar from her blouse, and left the place. She was going to talk to that tour guide if it was the last thing she did.

The tour had left from one of the popular voodoo shops along Rampart Street, not far from the hotel. Tessa figured that was as good a place to begin as any. When she stepped inside, she was surprised at the blast of cool air filling the place. It was a small shop, very high ceilings, walls of darkened wood. Every inch of it was lined in shelves loaded down with items. Voodoo dolls, candles in varying shapes and colors, cigars, and books and carved wooden images of tribal gods and Catholic saints, all mingled together. The air smelled of cigar smoke and incense. She walked up to the counter, looked at the girl behind it. "I'm wondering if you can help me find someone."

"If you want a reading, go through there," she said pointing to a doorway filled by beaded curtains. "Mamma Celia's in today. She's very good and she's free right now."

Tessa shook her head. "No, that's not what I meant.

I'm looking for someone specific. The tour guide, from the Haunted Tour that leaves from here?" "Which one? There are a dozen tour guides."

"He had long dark hair, ponytail, mustache and beard." She drew the pattern of his whiskers on her own face. "He wore these boots…."

"Oh, you mean Rudy. You don't know how many women used to come in here looking for him after a tour. But he don't work for us anymore. Hasn't in…oh, five years now."

"That's impossible. He guided the group I was in just last night."

The girl frowned over the glass counter at her until Tessa had to let her gaze fall. She found herself perusing the selection of tarot decks inside the case. "Do you know who did guide the nine-thirty tour group last night?" she asked.

"Lemme just check." The girl opened a book. "That would be Victor Carre."

"And do you know where I can find him?" she asked.

"He's leading another group in a half hour. He'll be out front a few minutes before then."

Tessa nodded her thanks and turned to go, but the rattling of the beaded curtains at the back of the room stopped her, and then a woman's voice said, "You, girl. Come. I need to read for you."

Tessa turned, stared at one of the most beautiful faces she had ever seen. The woman's brown eyes gleamed, and she reached for Tessa with a long, slender hand that bore rings on every finger and bracelets that jangled when she moved. She wore a silky turban of purple and blue. "I don't really want a reading," Tessa said.

"No matter. You need one. Come." And she drew Tessa back through the beaded curtains into a tiny room that smelled of sandalwood smoke.

5

"Sit, pretty one. Relax. There is nothing to fear."

The woman jingled as she moved around the small table in very cramped quarters, to sit in the chair on the other side. The table was draped in silk scarves in jewel colors. Candles lined the room, on the windowsill, and mounted in holders on the walls. There were at least a dozen of them burning, providing the only light in the place. Atop the scarves on the table, crystal stones were scattered about, and a deck of cards sat neatly stacked at the ready.

Tessa sat down in the chair opposite the woman. "Your name…no wait, don't tell me. It's…" She closed her eyes, a slow smile spreading over her face. "It's Marie."

Tessa's throat went dry. "It's Tessa. But I'm curious. What made you say Marie?"

"It's what spirit calls you, child. I have no idea why, but you own the name. Give me your hand." Her cool brown hand clasped Tessa's wrist, drawing it across the silk, palm up. She bent over for a closer look, the fingers of her free hand whispering over the lines in Tessa's palm. "You've lived many lives. In this one, they collide." She lifted her head. "You've spent a great deal of time in New Orleans. This city is in your blood."

"This is my first visit." The woman was so far off base Tessa wondered why her words were hitting her so hard, stirring up such odd feelings in her, making her want to nod and whisper, "Yes, yes, that's right" to everything she said.

"Interesting." She continued staring at Tessa's hand, then lifted her head to meet her eyes. "Why am I seeing fire?"

"Fire?"

She nodded. "As if your home has burned, and you with it."

Tessa jerked her hand away from the woman, jumping to her feet. "I have to go. I have to go now."

"Don't be silly, child, we haven't even consulted the cards yet."

"I have to go." She reached for her purse.

"No charge. Go. He's waiting for you."

She stared at the woman, but she was clearly finished with Tessa. She sat silently, contemplating a candle flame and idly shuffling her cards. Tessa hurried out through the beaded curtain, where the girl behind the counter smiled. "That was fast. Just as well, Victor's here." She nodded toward the doorway.

Tessa saw him from behind, the black coat was the same. Stiffening her spine, she went to him.

6

Tessa stepped out of the shop, and into a wall made of hot liquid air. Her shoes hit the sidewalk, and the tour guide turned to face her, and her stomach clenched.

But it wasn't him. This man was entirely different. Only the uniform was the same. He didn't even have the boots.

"I take it you're Victor?"

"I am. Are you here for the tour?"

She shook her head, left then right. "No. Actually, I took the tour last night. I need to speak with the man who guided it, but according to the girl in the shop, he hasn't worked as a tour guide for five years." His eyebrows went up and he glanced quickly around, as if to determine who was within earshot. "According to the books, you guided the tour I took last night," Tessa went on. "Only...you didn't."

The man gripped her upper arm, leading her a few steps farther from the open shop door. "Keep it down, okay? You're going to get me fired."

"I don't have any intention of causing you trouble, Victor. But I need to know who he was. And where I can find him."

He nodded quickly. "Look, he's a friend. He...was passing by when the tour group gathered, and all of the sudden he wanted to guide the tour." He shrugged. "I saw no harm in letting him take the group around for old times' sake. Hell, he knows the drill. I gave him 10 minutes to go change clothes, and then I let him have at it."

She nodded slowly. "Has he ever asked to take one of your groups before, since he quit working here?"

Victor shook his head slowly from side to side. "You're not going to turn me in, are you?"

"Not if you tell me where he lives," she said.

Victor looked her up and down, maybe trying to determine whether she could be any threat to his friend. He opened his mouth to speak, then closed it again. "I'll tell him you want to talk to him, see if it's okay with him for me to give out his number. Okay?"

She thought about threatening to turn him in, but then thought better of it. It would still be an option later. Besides, she didn't want to seem like some kind of stalker. "All right. I'm staying at the Rose." She took a pen and a scrap of paper from her bag and scrawled her name and room number. When should I expect your call?"

"Tonight, okay? I can't be more specific. He can be tough to reach."

"Okay." She nodded firmly. "Okay." Then she turned and continued her walk back to the hotel, a thousand questions spinning and whirling through her mind. She walked right past the shop on the corner, before remembering her film, and did a quick about-face to go pick up her photos. She paid for them, tucked the envelope into her bag and hurried across the street and a block up to her hotel. She took the antiquated elevator with its decorative gates, rode it up to the third floor, then got out and walked down the hall to the corner room, which was hers.

When she walked in, Tricia was just coming out of the bathroom, dressed in a white terry robe and toweling her hair. She met Tessa's eyes, and smiled. "Yes, I'm finally up. How was your morning?"

"It was...weird." She tossed her hat and glasses onto

the bed, then sat on the settee and tugged the photos out of her purse. "But I did get our pictures developed." She opened the envelope and began flipping through the shots while Tricia hurried to sit beside her to see.

Tessa flipped past the cemetery shots, the ones they'd taken at the Voodoo Museum, and then her hands came to a sudden frozen stop on a photo that she could not have taken. It was of the two of them, sound asleep in the twin beds of this very room.

7

"Oh, that's very funny, Tessa."

Tessa's hands were shaking. She couldn't take her eyes off the picture even to look at her sister.

"A good one. Really. You know I believe the stories about this place a little too much, so you have someone take pictures of us in bed sleeping. What am I supposed to think, that one of the ghosts did it?"

"Tricia…"

Tricia took the stack of photos from her sister's hands, going through them. "Oh, look there are more. This one was taken from the balcony, this one from over by the fireplace, and this one—oh, look at this one. From right beside your bed. Creepy, Tess."

"Tricia, shut the hell up."

Her sister stopped talking, and when Tessa looked at her she saw the smile die very slowly. "Come on, Tess, you're scaring me."

"I'm sorry. I put the camera on the nightstand last night. I thought there were several unexposed shots left on the roll, but when I took it out this morning, they'd all been used up."

"Tessa, this isn't funny."

"I know it isn't."

"Okay. Then…then someone's messing with us." Tricia swallowed hard. "I'm going to see the manager. If they think they can sneak around our rooms in the middle of the night just to perpetrate their ghost stories and increase business, they'd better think again." Tricia stomped back into the bathroom to put her clothes on.

But Tessa could only sit and stare at the final photograph in the stack. There was a mirror behind the bed, and while the camera had been aimed at her, herself, asleep, that mirror had been captured in the shot as well. And in it was a vague image in the darkness. A woman's face, all white, pale, and luminescent. Thin and transparent. It looked like Tessa's own face, painted in pale mists on the darkness.

8

The hotel management, naturally, denied any knowledge of the photos, or how they had come to be. Tricia said they had attempted to prove their case by showing her reams of videotape taken by the surveillance cameras in the third-floor hallway. No one had come in through the door all night.

That only left the balcony.

Tessa swallowed hard. "It's New Orleans. People party hard. Probably some kid decided to play a practical joke and climbed up the trellis or fire escape or something. I wouldn't worry about it."

"Maybe we should go to another hotel."

Tessa couldn't do that. She needed to be here, though she didn't know just why. "Everything's booked," she said softly. "I already checked." She realized that she had just done something she never, ever did. She had lied to her sister. She covered it quickly, plastering a smile onto her face. "Come on, let's go out. I want to take the trolley into the Garden District today, and explore. And at the end of the run there's a restaurant I want to try for dinner. Then we'll come back and go play at that karaoke bar on Bourbon Street, all right?"

"You're going to make me drop from sheer exhaustion before we get back home, aren't you?"

Tessa took her sister's hand. She really wished she could send her home, get her out of here. Something was going on, she could feel it right to her toes. She was coming alive inside, in ways she could not explain.

They toured, and walked, and took the obligatory photos of Anne Rice's house. They visited shops and museums and spent more money than was probably wise. They visited Lafayette Cemetery without a tour guide, something they had been warned not to do. While there, Tessa suffered a dizzy spell that left her weak and queasy. But she recovered soon enough, and blamed it on the heat. They walked along the sidewalks of Canal Street, looking up at the Mardi Gras beads that dangled from every tree and power line in sight, even months after the party. When they found some hanging low enough to reach, Tricia insisted on snatching them from the tree as a souvenir. Beads tossed during the parade were way better than the ones you could buy in any shop in New Orleans, she insisted. They had dinner very late, and then rode back to the French Quarter, and did some drinking and bar hopping on Bourbon Street.

When they finally returned to the hotel it was just after eleven, and the message light on the phone was blinking. Tricia didn't notice it as she headed straight for the shower. As soon as the water was running, Tessa picked up the phone and retrieved the message. Victor's tape-recorded voice played in her ear. "He says he'll meet you at midnight in the street below your balcony. That's the best I can do."

9

She waited until her sister was sound asleep, then slipped out of the room as quietly as she could manage. She hated leaving Tricia, knowing how nervous the room made her. Especially given the odd photos that had been taken of them sleeping last night. But she left the balcony doors open. If anything happened to frighten Tricia, Tessa would be able to hear her. And she could be at her side within a few seconds.

She tiptoed through the hall, took the stairs instead of the elevator, and then moved through the deserted lobby as soundlessly as if she were the ghost. When she opened the heavy, ornate wooden door, she could smell the night. She stepped out into its hot, sticky embrace, silently loving it. But there was no one in sight. Tessa walked a few steps along the sidewalk, looking in either direction, seeing no one. But then far in the distance, she heard the slow, steady clip-clop of hooves over stone.

Straining her eyes to see, she stared down the street, unsure of the direction, because the sound seemed to echo from everywhere at once. But then an ebony horse seemed to emerge from the darkness, slowly taking shape as it came closer. The carriage was as black as the horse that pulled it, covered and closed, not open like the buggies she'd seen traversing the Quarter by day. This was different.

Her heart hammered in her chest, and she couldn't seem to catch her breath as she stepped out of the street, up onto the sidewalk, and waited. It moved so slowly. As if the man in control was enjoying his power over her. Drawing her tension taut as a bowstring. Plucking it with every step of his horse's hooves. It was right in front of her now. The black horse stopped and shook its mane, tossing its head and blowing hot air from flared nostrils. The form sitting in the driver's seat, high above, was completely swathed in black. She couldn't even make him out.

Then the carriage's door swung open, and a deep, hauntingly familiar voice said, "Get in." She looked into the darkness inside the carriage. She couldn't see him. "I can't. I can't leave my sister alone in that room."

"It's not your sister the spirits want, Tessa. She'll sleep peacefully and undisturbed until you return."

"How can you be sure of that?" She blinked rapidly. "And…and how do you know my name?"

"I will answer all your questions if you will come with me."

"But—"

"Come." A gloved hand emerged from the inky darkness within the carriage, reached toward her and drew itself slowly back in. She felt as if it was pulling her along with it, and she obeyed, stepping into the carriage, into the heart of darkness. She got in, turning and sinking automatically into a soft velvet seat. The door slammed behind her, and the carriage lurched into motion as she looked up and straight into his eyes.

10

"I have waited a very long time for this night."

Swallowing her fear, Tessa held his piercing black gaze, unable to look away. He sat in the seat across from her, staring into her eyes. She felt him probing the depths of her mind, her soul, though she had no idea how. Why did just being near him make her tremble this way? Why?

"H-how could you have been waiting? You only met me two nights ago."

"We met more than a century ago."

She shook her head in denial, not questioning what he meant by that, maybe because she was afraid of what his answers would be. "I saw you last night. Below the balcony."

"And yet you didn't come to me. You wanted to. Why did you resist your own soul's yearnings, Tessa?"

Her stomach clenched into a knot. "I… Someone was in my room last night. Someone took photographs…."

"I know. I found a set of them in my bedroom this evening."

She blinked. "How could that be?"

"The spirits. The ghosts who haunt that hotel wanted me to find you. As if I wouldn't have known you from the moment I set eyes on you without their assistance."

"I don't know what you're talking about," she whispered.

"You will. Trust me, you will." He reached a hand across to her, touched her cheek with his gloved hand, gently brushing her hair aside, and as he did, his eyes fell closed and a sigh stuttered from his lips. "Will you do me the honor of sitting here beside me?"

She blinked at him in the darkness, then at the seat he patted.

"I mean you no harm, Tessa, I swear it on my soul. But if I can't touch you soon I think I may die."

"T-touch me?" Her heart slammed her rib cage as if trying to break free.

"Hold you. Close to me. That's all." He drew an unsteady breath. "Please?"

She wanted nothing more than to feel him touching her. As the carriage rocked, she changed seats, joining him on the softness, sitting very close to his side. Her body stiffened in anticipation as he slid an arm around her shoulders, and then he sighed softly, leaning back, pulling her closer, so that she lay cradled in his arms, her head on his shoulder. With his free hand he stroked her hair. "Promise me something, ma cherie," he whispered. "Promise me you will hear the story I have to tell you, all of it, before you make a choice."

"A choice?"

His crooked finger came beneath her chin, lifting it, turning her face up to his. "Yes, there will be a choice. One that will alter your life forever. But not yet. Not yet."

His lips were so close to hers she could feel the breath of each word. She wanted him to kiss her. She felt it suddenly, with everything in her. More than she wanted to draw another breath, she wanted to feel his lips on hers.

As if he knew her every thought, he bent just a little closer.

11

His lips brushed across hers, and every nerve in her body came to life at the sweet, brief contact. But then the carriage came to a halt, and he drew away. "Come. We are here."

"Where?"

"Lafayette Cemetery. You were here today, but you didn't see what you came to see. I thought you might stumble upon it. Led, perhaps, by sheer instinct. But, no. Perhaps you were not ready."

She remembered the dizzy, sick feeling that had swamped her when she'd visited this place before. He got to his feet and climbed out of the carriage, reaching back in for her. He took her hand, helped her down. She felt oddly out of place in her jeans and simple blouse.

She felt as if she should be wearing a bustled gown with a matching hat. He led her through the opening in the wall that surrounded the cemetery. Every tomb was a small crypt. No one was buried here, she had read, because the water table was simply too high. Instead the graves were above ground, tiny cement tombs with peaked roofs, ornate with carved angels or crosses, names arching across the tops. Rows of them, like miniature villages. Villages of the dead. He led her between the rows, toward the very depths of the place, the center, and there he showed her a tall narrow crypt. The name across the top was "Lemieux."

Underneath were two other names. Marcus and Marie.

Tessa stared up at him, blinking, feeling a bit of the same dizziness she had felt here before. "The artist and the prostitute?"

"Then you know something of them already."

She felt a death chill, standing there staring at a cement crypt that held the remains of a woman who could have been her twin. "I picked up the book. The one you wanted me to pick up. I read about them."

"The book only tells you part of the story."

"But you're going to tell me the rest?"

He nodded. "Marcus was an artist. His father was

a French noble who was driven out of his country in shame, and came to live here because it reminded him of home. But he lived in constant fear of being shamed again."

She looked at her tour guide, into his eyes. "What shamed him in France?"

"He was cuckolded. His wife ran away with a commoner. It was the talk of Paris at the time. Quite the scandal. He was a proud man, too proud to live that way, so he came here, where he was treated almost as royalty."

"And then his son fell in love with a prostitute."

"The father forbade it, of course. Still, Marcus was a stubborn man. And he loved her deeply. Painted her often. He would sit for hours just staring at her image, when he couldn't be with her. Some said he was obsessed, others that she had bewitched him."

"He was in love," Tessa whispered.

"Madly in love. They were secretly wed. Marcus had only to collect his things, slip away with a horse and a carriage, and pick her up. They were to run away together that very night."

"The night of the fire?" Tessa asked, her breath catching in her throat.

Staring into her eyes, he nodded. "Marcus arrived to see the entire building engulfed in flames. He could hear his Maria's screams." He lowered his head, shuddering, and Tessa thought there were tears in his eyes.

12

"He went inside to try to get her out," Tessa said, filling in the parts of the heartbreaking story that she already knew.

"Yes. But it was too late. He was nearly killed himself. Neighbors, firefighters, they came, pulled him out of the fire, doused him in water, saving his life. But he screamed, begged them to let him die with the woman he loved."

Tessa's eyes were wet now, her throat tight. "Marie died."

"Yes. But there was another woman there that night. The most powerful woman in New Orleans, watching, weeping. Marie St. Claire's mother had named her for this woman, because she had been unable to conceive a child until the elder Marie helped her."

"The elder Marie?"

He nodded, his eyes intense. "Yes. Marie LaVeau."

Tessa blinked in shock, backing up a step. "This is getting very difficult to believe."

"Why?" he asked. "It shouldn't. Helping barren women to conceive was a common request of voodoo practitioners. LaVeau was a queen, the best known, most in demand. And she was good at what she did. The woman had real power. Real power."

"How do you know?" Tessa whispered.

He met her eyes. "Because I'm here. And you're here. It's just as she told me it would be."

Blinking, Tessa shook her head. "Marie LaVeau died long before you were born."

He shook his head slowly. "She was there that night," he said. "And she shouted her curse and her blessing. She put her hands on Marcus, who was so distraught he was barely aware of the damage the fire had done to him, to his hands and arms."

Tessa nodded. "I read that he could never paint again."

"For a long time, he couldn't. And by the time he

could, he no longer wanted to. His inspiration, his muse, had been consumed by fire."

Tessa swallowed back her tears. "What was Marie LaVeau's curse?"

"Whether it was curse or blessing remains to be seen," he said. "She raised up her hands, tipped back her head, and shouted above the roar of the flames and the cries of the dying, 'My namesake shall live again! And her lover will live as well, never to age, nor die, nor leave this city, until that time when she returns to him and they find the love that was stolen from them this cursed night!' Then she howled like the very voice of death."

Tessa imagined she could hear the sound. There was wind, where there had been none before, and it seemed to carry that ghostly wail.

"The younger Marie's cries stopped, dying with the witch's howl," Marcus said. "Most believe she died at that very moment, only able to release her hold on life once she had the promise that she would find her love again." He lowered his head. "Then LaVeau went to Marcus, embraced him, and whispered that he must be strong, that he must be patient. She told him the other women who had died in the fire would guard the place as sacred, and would see to it that he knew when his wife returned for him." He looked Tessa in the eyes.

"That's why they took the photos, and brought them to me, you see. To let me know that you had finally come back."

13

He was holding her hands in his, staring deeply into her eyes. A passing breeze gently dried the dampness from her skin and her cheeks. She said, "What are you talking about? I'm not Marie."

"No, you are Tessa. But in that lifetime, you were Marie. My precious Marie."

She blinked, not understanding. "You're talking about reincarnation?"

"Yes. Of course."

"Then you…you believe that you were reincarnated, too? That you were Marcus in that lifetime?" She knew the answer to the question before she asked it. Before he slowly shook his head left and then right.

"I told you LaVeau's curse. That Marcus would live

on, would never age, not until his Marie returned. And now you have."

"Are you saying that you are Marcus? That you never died, that you've been living here waiting for me for more than a hundred years?"

"One hundred fifty-one years, two months, fifteen days." He glanced at the watch he wore. "Seventeen and a half minutes." When he looked at her face again, his wore a slight smile, sad humor tingeing his eyes. But when he saw the doubt in hers, his smile died. "I can prove it to you, my love. Please, you must give me that chance."

Shaking her head, stepping backward again, she said, "I think I've had enough for one night. I'd like to go back to the hotel now."

He closed his eyes, lowered his head. "You're afraid of me now. You think me insane."

"I'm sorry, I—"

He held up a hand. "No. It's all right. I should have expected it. The story is far-fetched, particularly in this age when magic is seen as impossible superstition."

"It's just that—at the voodoo shop they told me your name was Rudy."

He nodded. "I have changed my name many times. I've had to leave here for years at a time, although thanks to Madame LaVeau's curse, I could never go far. But I would go into hiding and return years later, pretending to be another of my own relatives, taking up residence again in the family home, using another name."

She blinked, her head spinning. "And what about the tomb? It has your name on it."

"Look closer." He ran his hand over the woman's name, the dates carved beneath it. Born 1827, Died 1850. Then his own, or the name he claimed as his own. It had a date of birth, 1825, but there was no date of death chiseled into granite.

Swallowing hard, she lifted her gaze to his face. "I'm sorry. Even with that, it's just too much to believe."

"I know. But there is one more thing I can show you...." Holding up his left hand, he slowly peeled off the glove that he wore to cover it. Clouds skittered away from the face of the moon, allowing its milky light to spill down on the badly scarred hand he held up before her. And even as she watched with her breath caught in her throat, he peeled off the other glove to reveal the right hand, which was even more damaged than the left.

14

"Oh my God." She backed away from him, then turning, she ran through the darkness, along the row of tombs. She darted to the left, then right, running full speed, having no idea which way to turn. She couldn't see beyond a few concrete crypts in any direction. Only those dark shadowy peaks in the village of the dead. Finally, she stopped, breathless, panting, more light-headed than before.

"I've frightened you."

The words came from behind her, making her jump and spin around.

"It's the last thing I wanted to do, Marie."

"Tessa! My name is Tessa."

He closed his eyes, lowered his head. "I know, I'm

sorry. Forgive me, I…" He pressed a hand, gloved again now, to his forehead, rubbing slow circles there. "To me you are one and the same."

"But not to me."

"I'll try to remember that." He lifted his gaze, met her eyes. "Come back to the carriage. I'll return you to the hotel."

She hesitated, watching him, painfully aware of how alone she was here, how difficult it would be to summon help. There were houses nearby, yes. Wealthy homes so large and well built she doubted anyone within them would hear her cries for help even if she screamed with everything in her. And even if they did, how could help find her in this maze, in time to prevent—

"You have nothing to fear from me, Tessa," he assured her yet again. "I would die for you. Nearly did, once. Would have if the others hadn't pulled me from the flames."

She licked her lips, lowered her head. "You do realize that what you're saying is impossible. You would be nearly two hundred years old."

"Nothing is impossible, Tessa. I've learned that over the years."

She shook her head in denial.

"You've been drawn to me since you first set eyes on

me, when I saw you and took over the tour group that night. You couldn't explain why, but you couldn't get me out of your mind."

She held his gaze, saying nothing. Finally, he sighed, lowering his head. "I'm pushing too hard, too soon." He looked up, past her left shoulder. "The carriage is that way. Come." Then he walked past her, easily locating the open part in the wall, beyond which that black carriage sat in the street, its shrouded driver sitting at the ready.

Marcus, or whatever his name was, went to it, opened the door for her. "Good night, Tessa."

"You're not riding along?" She stood between his body and the open door, staring into his eyes because she couldn't seem to do otherwise.

"I've frightened you enough for one night. I would ask one promise of you, though I realize I have no right to ask anything at all."

"What promise?"

"Don't leave New Orleans without…at least saying goodbye." He had a card in his hand, which he tucked into her jeans pocket.

She bit her lip, nodded. "I suppose…that's not so much to ask."

"And…"

"And?"

"And this…" Leaning closer, he curled his arms around her waist, pulled her tight against him, and kissed her.

15

Tessa's mind told her she should be deeply offended. She should feel violated. She should tear herself free of his embrace, slap him, upbraid him for the uninvited invasion.

Why, then, was she kissing him instead? Why had her arms twisted around his neck, her fingers twined in his hair as her mouth made love to his? Why were there tears running down her cheeks while her entire body trembled?

One salty tear reached her lips, and his, she thought, because he broke the kiss abruptly, blinking down at her, concern etched on his face. "Tessa?" he asked.

Shaking her head violently, she climbed into the carriage and tugged the door closed behind her. The vehicle rocked into motion, and she buried her face in her hands, weeping softly all the way back to the hotel.

She had no idea why being in his arms had felt like a long-awaited homecoming. She had no idea why it had nearly broken her heart to leave him there, alone, in the night. It wasn't as if she believed any part of his story. It was sad, heart-wrenching, and it touched her, but it wasn't real. It couldn't be real.

She got out of the carriage as soon as it stopped, and it set into motion once more the moment her feet touched the street. She didn't bother looking after it. Instead she hurried inside, rubbing her tears from her face on her way up the stairs, and finally reached the haven of her room. She dug in a pocket for the key, but as she lifted it toward the lock, the door swung slowly open.

Catching her breath, she looked up and saw her sister standing there. Only—it wasn't. Her face was pale, and her eyes—her eyes were the wrong color. They were jet black, with a soft glowing light coming from within them.

"You must remember. You must," she said in a voice that was not her own.

"Tricia?"

"Unless you remember, it was all for nothing,"

Tricia went on in that strange voice. Then she reached up, her hands clasping Tessa's shoulders like claws. "Remember!" she shouted, shaking her violently, with surprising strength. "Remember, damn you!"

"Tricia!" Tessa planted her palms flat on her sister's chest and shoved with everything in her. Tricia's grip was broken, and she staggered backward.

"Remember," she whispered, and then she collapsed on the floor.

16

Tessa rushed forward to help her possessed sister, falling to her knees beside her. "Tricia. Tricia, come on, wake up!" She lifted Tricia's upper body, patting her cheeks. "Come on, wake up."

Tricia's eyes fluttered open, and she stared up at her sister. "What? What's wrong?"

"You were…uh, sleepwalking. Or something."

"I was?" Tricia sat up, looking around the room. "Wow, I ended up on the floor huh? Geez, that's odd. I never sleepwalk."

"You don't…remember anything?"

"No. Nothing." She smiled at her sister. "Hey, you're still dressed."

"Couldn't sleep," she said. She wondered if her sister

would notice the door standing open behind her and ask where she had been, but when she glanced at it with the thought, she saw that the door was closed.

"Come on," Tessa said, helping her sister to her feet. "Let's get you back into bed." She shook off the feeling that someone else was in the room with them, or had been. She told herself she must have closed the door herself. But she knew right then what she had to do.

She had to get the hell out of New Orleans. As soon as possible. This was no longer just affecting her, it was getting to her sister, and she would not allow that.

She didn't sleep that night. She did put on a nightgown and slide into bed, but she never closed her eyes. She sat awake to protect her younger sister from whatever might be lingering in this place. There was something. God, it made no sense to her. She didn't believe in ghosts, but she could feel them with every cell in her body. She could almost hear them whispering to her. "Remember."

In the morning, over breakfast in The Rose's dining room. She tried to put on a carefree expression as she told her sister, "Honey, how do you feel about expanding our vacation a little bit?"

"Like—how?" Tricia asked. She seemed none the worse for wear. Her appetite was good, while Tessa found herself unable to choke down a bite of the luscious omelet or the delectable pastries. She could barely swallow the coffee and it was the best she had ever had.

"Let's get out of New Orleans," she said. "Let's rent a car and go driving out into the countryside. We can tour some of the old plantations, take a look around the bayou, maybe visit some of the historic battlefields."

Tricia frowned, tilting her head to one side. "But there's still so much we haven't seen right here," she said. "Honey, you're not getting all wigged out about the ghost stories in this place, are you? I mean, my sleepwalking last night probably had more to do with the spicy meals we've been eating than with any ghosts."

Lowering her head, Tessa said, "I just don't like it here. I need to get out, Trish."

Her sister frowned. "All right, if you feel that strongly about it." She tucked into her omelet with relish, and didn't bring the subject up again.

17

Tessa hurried to make arrangements, using the phone in the room while her sister flipped through the pages of the entertainment guide. Trish looked up only when Tessa slammed the receiver down with an aggravated sigh.

"What's wrong?"

"It seems the entire universe is conspiring to keep us here."

"Permanently?" Tricia asked, a mischievous eyebrow arching in question.

"Every car rental place I called is booked. The earliest we can get a car is first thing tomorrow morning. And the innkeeper insists twenty-four hours' notice is required in order to check out early—if we leave today, we get billed for tonight anyway."

Tricia shrugged. "Maybe we should stay then. Hell, Tess, one more night won't kill us."

Tessa licked her lips.

"Besides, look what's opening tonight at the Saenger Theatre." She handed to Tessa the paper she'd been reading, and Tess saw the half page ad. A production of The Phantom of the Opera. Oh, hell, it couldn't have been anything else. Her sister was a Phantom-nut. She had collectibles, CDs of the music, playbills from every production of the show she had seen, and that was no small number.

"Come on, sis. Just one more night? We'll leave first thing in the morning."

Tessa sighed. "I don't feel good about this, Trish."

"Tess, this is my vacation, too. But if you feel that strongly, go ahead. You go on ahead without me. I'll see the show, spend one last night here, and meet you wherever you say in the morning. Okay?"

Tessa looked up fast with wide eyes. "I can't leave you here alone!"

Tricia frowned deeply. "Are you sure you're feeling okay?"

She shook her head rapidly. "Fine, fine, you win.

One more night. But we're out of here in the morning, all right?"

"Okay." Tricia smiled. "Meanwhile, I've made us lunch reservations at Emeril's place. And there's a museum we haven't visited yet. They have a special exhibit featuring the work of Marcus Lemieux. I was reading about him in that book you bought yesterday. He's the artist who was involved with that prostitute who died in the fire here."

Closing her eyes slowly, Tessa nodded, fingering the card she held in her pocket, racked with guilt for her intent to break her promise, and already having second thoughts.

18

Tessa gritted her teeth with expectation when they went to see Marcus's display at the museum, but she was relieved that not one painting of that long-dead woman she so resembled was included in the exhibit. She wondered why, but then she knew. Marie's paintings were private. He had probably kept them. Maybe they still hung in the home of the beautiful Lemieux descendant who called himself Marcus.

She knew, suddenly, that they did. That he spent hours staring at them, longing for the woman they depicted. No wonder he'd become obsessed to the point of delusion.

The work on display touched her. A mother, holding the hand of a small child. Two lovers, on a bench beneath the moonlight, entwined in a gentle embrace. A church, with flowering wisteria creeping up its outer walls.

She walked with her sister, admiring the work, then suddenly stopped and sucked in a breath, her hand flying to her chest as if to still her pounding heart.

It was the self-portrait. For an instant she had thought she'd rounded the corner and come face-to-face with him. But she hadn't. It was only a portrait, life-size, and accurate to a fault. His eyes seemed to stare at her, so filled with sadness she nearly wept.

"Hey, doesn't this look a lot like that tour guide you were so into the other night?"

Tessa nodded, but found herself unable to speak. She couldn't tug her eyes from his. God, she couldn't leave without saying goodbye. She just couldn't.

That night, after her sister left for the theater, Tessa pulled the card from her pocket, and with hands that shook violently, she picked up the telephone and dialed the number on the card.

His voice when he answered was soft and deep, and achingly familiar. It caressed her ear when he whispered her name, knowing who was calling before she told him. "Tessa?"

"Yes, it's me," she said. "I…I'm keeping my promise. To let you know before I left New Orleans."

"You're leaving?"

God, the pain contained in those two simple words. "I have to. I'm sorry."

"When?"

"In the morning."

There was a long moment of silence. Then he said, "I'll come to you then. Tonight."

"Marcus, I don't think that's such a good idea. This is already difficult enough, and I—"

"God help me, Tessa, but I can't let you go without seeing you one more time. Please, say you'll see me tonight."

She hesitated.

"Please…"

"All right." It made no sense, but she could hardly speak around the lump in her throat, and she was as desperate to see him again as he seemed to be to see her. "Outside the hotel, just as before?"

"Yes. I'll wait beneath the balcony."

"I'll come down," she said. "Is an hour too soon?" Did that sound as eager to his ears as it had to her own?

"More likely too long," he told her. "I'll be there soon. And Tessa?"

"Yes?"

"I love you."

19

Tessa told herself it was insane to fuss, but she couldn't seem to help herself. She chose a dress that was flowing and white and mostly sheer. It looked Grecian, and she'd always loved it. She took it into the bathroom with her, hung it on a rack while she stepped into the shower, and rinsed away the dust and sweat of a day's touring. And if her heart and her body tingled in anticipation, she couldn't help it. This thing had moved beyond her control. This was the last time she would see him. She was doing the right thing. Surely that was good enough to appease the practical, logical part of her mind. Surely she could at least enjoy this one, final encounter.

Finished in the shower, she stepped out, toweled down, and pulled on the dress. It was soft on her skin.

Then she leaned over the bathroom mirror to arrange her damp hair. She pinned it up loosely, letting tendrils fall around her face and tickle her neck and shoulders. Then she applied makeup.

But almost as soon as she began, the light in the bathroom flickered out.

Frowning, Tessa flipped it on and off several times, then tried the other lights in the room to no avail. Snatching up the phone, she dialed the front desk.

"Just a brief outage," the manager promised her. "It happens from time to time. Feel free to use the oil lamp on the mantel until we get it fixed."

She hung up, went to the oil lamp, found the matches beside it, and set the thing alight. By its light she glanced at her watch. Only minutes until he was due to arrive. She hurried back into the bathroom, taking the lamp with her, and put the finishing touches on her face.

Then she carried the lamp back to the bedroom, set it on the mantel, and went to the French doors. Stepping out onto the balcony, she looked at the street below.

He was there. He looked up at her, met her eyes, lifted a hand toward her in greeting.

"I'll be right down," she called softly. And she knew he heard her, knew he would know she had taken pains to look beautiful for him, and she didn't care.

She turned and walked back into the room. But when she had gone no more than four steps, the French doors slammed behind her. Tessa jumped in alarm, turning back to stare. "What in the world?" She went back, reached for the handles, tugged on them, but they wouldn't budge. Suddenly frightened, she crossed the room to the only other exit, the one that led into the hall.

But when she tugged, that door wouldn't open either.

Turning, facing the room's center, she looked around her. "What's going on? Please, just tell me what you want from me!"

The oil lamp floated from the mantel to the center of the room, hovering there.

"Remember!" a woman's voice demanded. Then the lamp was hurled by unseen hands. It exploded on the floor in a pool of yellow fire.

20

Tessa ran forward, yanking a blanket from the bed, and trying to use it to douse the fire. But the flames spread unnaturally, slowly surrounding her. She stumbled toward the French doors, reaching for them, but she couldn't get past the wall of fire, even to hurl herself through the glass.

She shrieked in terror. And then, through the curtain of fire, she saw him on the street below, the horror in his face as he realized what was happening. She saw him racing toward the building to come for her, and suddenly it all returned.

Everything. Her love for him. God, it was an all-consuming, all-powerful love. His father, yes. Yes, it was his father who had started the fire all those years ago. She'd seen him leaving, but it was too late. Already the flames had been licking around her bed. She'd tried so hard to escape. To get to Marcus. Tried so hard to cling to life, even as the fire seared her flesh.

The flames raged higher, engulfing the room. The windows exploded. She screamed and screamed, and she no longer knew which parts of this night were happening now, and which were parts of her memory.

But the pain was so great, so intense. Her hair was on fire, her dress blazing, her skin melting from the bones and yet she clung to life. For him. For Marcus.

And then she heard a voice shouting from the streets far below. It was the voice of the woman who had read her palm in the little voodoo shop. And yet it was a voice she knew from another lifetime. The voice of Marie LaVeau.

"My namesake shall live again! And her lover will live as well, never to age, nor die, nor leave this city, until that time when she returns to him and they find the love that was stolen from them this cursed night!" Then her cry echoed through Tessa's mind and she knew it was time to let go of the pain, to leave the agonizing prison of her body, to move on. And she could, but only because she knew she would come back again.

She would return to Marcus one day. And he would be right there waiting when she did.

She closed her eyes, and sank to the floor amid the flames.

Two things woke her. The first was the feeling of water spraying her face, cool, blessed water. The second was the sound of the door being kicked in.

Tessa opened her eyes. She was lying on the floor in the center of her room. The sprinklers in the ceiling were dousing her and the entire place with water. And then Marcus was there, on his knees beside her, cradling her in his arms.

"I thought I saw flames. My God, are you all right?"

Thought he saw flames? But the entire room had gone up... Sitting up, blinking, Tessa looked around. There was a small ring of black on the floor where the oil from the lamp had spread, and burned. But nothing else in the room was damaged. Not the curtains or the bedding. The windows were intact. Even the dress Tessa wore was perfectly unharmed.

Marcus was stroking her damp hair away from her face. "Tell me you're all right, my love, please."

"I'm all right," she whispered, staring up into his eyes, paying no attention to the others in the room, the hotel staff, and some firefighters who had just arrived. "More than that, Marcus, my beloved Marcus...I remember."

He searched her face, her eyes, his own filling with moisture. "You remember?"

"It's been so long, my love, so long. I love you. I love you, Marcus."

He gathered her close, and kissed her as his tears of joy spilled over. And Tessa knew that she would never, ever be apart from him again. Neither in this lifetime, nor those to come.

* * * * *

Edge of Craving

RHYANNON BYRD

1

Southern Wales, early 1800's

How could such an angelic smile be cast upon a monster?

The whispered words wormed their way through Rhys's mind as he watched Alia Buchanan, daughter of the Merrick scholar he'd been charged to protect, make her way across the flagstone-covered courtyard. A lavender twilight was falling heavily over the hilltop where the ivy-covered Buchanan cottage sat nestled amidst the surrounding forest, the autumn air scented with the compelling blend of wood smoke and a distant storm rumbling on the horizon. Smoky shafts of purple and blue touched their fingers to the delicate angles of the young woman's face, lingering over the gentle swell of her breasts…the long, flowing locks of her hair. If he wanted to retain his sanity, Rhys knew he needed to look away. And yet his eyes refused to obey the command, riveted to the sight of her mysterious expression as their gazes locked, then held, that soft, breathtaking smile still curving the sensual shape of her mouth.

No matter how distant he tried to be—no matter how rude or how savagely he scowled *and* glared—she always gifted him with that same goddamn, infuriating smile. And it was slowly driving him out of his mind, the threads of his sanity slipping through his fingers like spiraling streams of mist. No matter how hard he struggled, he could *not* catch them in his grasp.

Since the moment he'd first been introduced to Alia, Rhys had been obsessed with her. An unusual situation for a warrior who had never found himself fascinated with anything or anyone, much less a whimsical slip of a girl he could too easily break beneath his power and his strength. The Merrick blood of her ancestors—one of the original ancient, nonhuman clans—had been dormant in her bloodline for generations, leaving Alia and her father with bodies that were as vulnerable as any human's. It was madness for him to even contemplate touching her, much less for him to fantasize about her to the point that she was a constant, aching presence within his mind.

But he couldn't stop. And God only knew that he'd tried.

If it had simply been her physical appearance that enthralled him, he could have found a way to see reason and put her out of his thoughts. After all, he'd always been of the opinion that one pretty face could be easily replaced by another. But there was so much more to the *pull* that kept drawing him to Alia, despite how hard he tried to resist. She was too intoxicating…too fresh. He could only marvel at how she viewed the world, seeing it in a way that he was sure no one else did. Seeing it through eyes that could pierce and penetrate, slipping beneath even the most hardened, belligerent defenses. That was how he felt now, holding her dark blue gaze, the uncomfortable sensation swarming through his veins, giving him the impression that she could see *him* in a way that no one else ever would.

He'd have attributed the odd sensation to the fact that she was descended on her mother's side from a power-ful line of Reavess witches, but knew that it was more than that. There was something about Alia herself that resonated with him, allowing her to slip under his guard, drawing his attention again and again. Consuming his waking moments. Tormenting his dreams.

Despite the coldness in his soul, her smiles always swept through the icy depths of Rhys's body like intoxicating, melting waves of heat, igniting a dangerous craving for things he could never have. With nothing more than that soft tilting of her mouth, the longing sincerity of her beautiful gaze, she warmed a place within him that had never been more than a barren, desolate sheet of ice. Ironic, really, considering he was a thing of fire himself. As one of the few remaining descendants of the Charteris, one of the original and rare European dragon clans, Rhys's body held the power to become a lethal source of heat. A dangerous, deadly power that only intensified as his attraction to a woman grew stronger—and one that was capable of melting Alia Buchanan alive if he were to ever sink inside the lush, delicate depths of her feminine little body.

He craved her. Craved everything about her, from her scent to her taste to the thoughts that filled her head.

And that was why he couldn't have her.

She was forbidden fruit that was going to get him into trouble, and he knew it. Had known it from the second he'd first laid eyes upon her five months ago, when he'd been sent to oversee her father's protection. And yet

Rhys could *not* take his gaze from her lithe, graceful form as she walked across the courtyard where he and four of his men had been vigorously training.

How in God's name was he supposed to stop watching the sweetest, most beautiful thing he'd ever seen? Heart-shaped face. Impish freckles. Light brown hair that couldn't decide between golden honey and autumn red. She was beautiful and wild, like an ancient goddess come to life. Her slim, winged brows swept over big, exotic eyes of a deep dark blue that reminded him of clear mountain skies. Full, pink mouth that made a man's mind slip into explicit imaginings of what it would be like to sink past those glistening lips and seek the damp, warm heat within.

Though he'd done his best to understand his infatuation, he was no closer to comprehending why he couldn't get her out of his mind than he was to knowing why she always smiled at him so sweetly—but then, his entire world had been off-kilter since coming to guard Matthew Buchanan. He was certain of only one thing—that he needed to end his obsession with the man's daughter before it sent him reeling into insanity.

As if to tempt him beyond endurance, she chose to move in his direction as she made her way around the courtyard fountain, its gurgling rush of water often soothing Rhys in the cold hours of the night when he would stand in the shadows and watch her window, waiting for a glimpse of her profile as she prepared for bed. Her path brought her closer to where he stood with his sword still gripped in his hand, her scent carried to his nose by the gentle breeze, and he clenched his free hand into a hard fist as the warm, sensual fragrance of jasmine overwhelmed his senses. Her smile melted into his body, under his skin, making him uncomfortable and hot. Making something in his chest go *tight*. It made no sense for her to waste that sweet, endearing expression on someone like him. Too often, women turned away from him in fear or unease—not that he blamed them. He was too big. Too scarred and hard and dark. Too goddamn scary looking.

And yet, as she moved past him, her soft, sweet smile seemed to be filled with a deep, desperate longing that matched his own.

You fool, he silently sneered. *Angels don't yearn for monsters.*

Forcing himself to turn his back on her, he stiffly spun around, the wind chilly against his face now that her smile no longer warmed him. Doing his best not to breathe in her scent, Rhys stared out over the verdant valley below. All looked calm…peaceful, and yet he had the strangest premonition of doom. Of evil rolling in on the cool, crisp breeze. With a deep scowl settling between his brows, he stared over the endless rolling hills of green, searching for the unknown threat. Despite the fact that the months he'd spent there had been quiet, Rhys knew the circumstances could change at any moment. Buchanan's work was so secret, few of the Consortium—the body of leaders who governed the remaining ancient clans—even knew of his research, or the fact that Rhys and his men were there to protect the father and daughter, but that didn't mean the danger was any less real.

Before he'd been sent to the remote hilltop in Wales, Rhys had been told in secret that the Merrick scholar was working to uncover the hidden location of the ancient Consortium archives, which had been lost hundreds of years before, when the leaders had been hunted down and massacred by the human mercenaries who called themselves the Collective Army. The Collective was dedicated to destroying all preternatural life, which meant they too would be searching for the lost archives believed to hold the secrets of every ancient clan in existence. With the archives, they believed they could find the nesting grounds of each remaining clan and finally purge the earth of them once and for all.

But the Collective weren't the only ones who would want to get their hands on the archives before the new Consortium could. Though for the most part the remaining ancient clans lived in peace with the humans, there were still those who dwelled in the shadows of darkness. Those who would seek the information in the archives to further their own dark agendas, whatever they might be. Rhys didn't concern himself with the whys. As a member of the Consortium's private guard, he protected without question those who needed protection, which was why he was there. A little more than five months ago, Matthew Buchanan had apparently made a significant discovery after a trip that took him south to Somerset, then east to London, before he returned home again to Wales. Rhys had not been told the nature of the discovery, but he knew that it was the reason behind the Consortium's decision to increase Buchanan's protection, assigning a full unit of guards to the cottagehold. And while the summer had passed quietly, Rhys couldn't help but believe that something was brewing.

"Are you going to continue staring out over the valley, or are we actually going to finish this exercise?" a deep voice drawled from behind him. Turning, he found Barrett leaning his left shoulder against the stone wall that lined the east and west sides of the courtyard, a wry smile tipping the corner of the soldier's mouth. A self-proclaimed "mongrel," Barrett's bloodline held so many different strains of nonhuman blood, he'd been left with bits and pieces of traits from each. He had an excellent sense of smell, as well as keen night vision, both of which made him an exceptional tracker. He was also strong, and fast, which made him one of the best sparring partners Rhys had ever had. Too often, the men in his command weren't able to keep up with him during practice, his strength and speed too much for them.

Sparring with Barrett now would no doubt be a good release of the tension in his muscles, but it wasn't going to help with the dangerous thoughts creeping through his mind. Slipping his sword back into the sheath that hung from the wide leather belt at his waist, Rhys met his friend's curious gaze. "I believe we've trained enough for the day."

"I thought that might be the case," Barrett murmured, his dark gaze shifting to the setting sun as it melted into the horizon, the tight expression on his lean face making Rhys wonder what he was thinking. He'd have asked what was troubling Barrett, but his own thoughts were mired in turmoil and confusion. He was too restless to stand there and talk. He needed to get away...to escape, and it crossed his mind that he should head into the local village of Wolcott and find a woman to at least sate his lust and get his bloody mind off Alia, if only for a few moments.

Go to the village. Go, goddamn it, before it's too late.

He scowled, suddenly turning to head into the forest before he could change his mind, thinking that the long walk would do him good, but Barrett's grip on his arm pulled him back around. "Heading to the village?" his friend asked, releasing his hold, the knowing look in Barrett's eyes telling Rhys that the man already knew exactly where he was going. And why. "I was going to suggest it myself. A big of a diversion will be good for you, Rhys. You look...tense. Best work out some of that aggression in a more natural way," he drawled, "than taking it out on the rest of us."

Rhys arched one brow at the grinning ass. "What are you complaining about? You're still in one piece."

Barrett's white teeth flashed in a crooked smile. "I've faired all right, so far. But the others are growing weary of their injuries. 'Tis the truth that you're growing more...aggressive every day and the others are growing weary of their injuries."

Shaking his head at the soldier's teasing, Rhys said, "Just make sure that the men stay sharp," and then he turned away. Raking one hand through his hair, he ground his jaw and once again forced himself to head toward the forest, in the direction of the village. It might leave a sour taste in his mouth, but he badly needed a distraction, just as Barrett had suggested. And while Rhys knew his trip to Wolcott wouldn't ease his dark, insatiable craving for the innocent Alia, he prayed that he would at least be able to find a fleeting moment of peace whilst there.

2

As soon as Alia turned the corner, she leaned against the chilled wall of the cottage, one hand pressed to her belly, the other pressed against her chest. It'd been so hard to keep calm as Rhys had watched her make her way across the courtyard, the heat from that cool, pale gaze enough to make her skin damp…her heart race. Closing her eyes, she struggled to breathe down the crazy rush of sensation still pounding its way through her system.

Unable to help herself, she peeked back around the corner, just needing to soak in the breathtaking visual he made once more. He wore his thick, dark hair shorter than the other soldiers, but still long enough that the wavy strands spilled wild in the wind, begging for the touch of her fingers. His body was overwhelmingly large and powerful, telling the tale of his life as a warrior. Pale, silvery scars covered his dark skin, marking his arms and hands, as well as his beautiful, strong-featured face. Once, she'd even seen him training with his men without a shirt on, and her heart had broken at the sight of his abused back. At the thick, tangled scars that raised its surface.

He was wrapped up in black, from his boots to his shirt, same as he always was. The midnight color should have looked severe, but it somehow seemed perfectly fitting for Rhys. He didn't need any color or adornment to make him more attractive. He was already too appealing as it was.

And then there were those eyes. Pale, wintry gray eyes. They should have looked cold…barren, and yet they somehow smoldered with heat, as if lit within by a burning flame. A spark of fire that turned the pale gray to molten silver, reminding her of the starry night.

There was so much bleak, wrenching loneliness in his eyes; it sometimes hurt just to look at them. She couldn't help but want to change that for him. She wanted to bring sunshine and happiness to his dark existence. Wanted to hear him laugh, to be surrounded by the deep, rich rumble of sound as it broke from his chest.

She wanted to see the bright, burning spark of joy in those soulful eyes, and know that he was at peace. That he felt loved…cherished. She wanted so much for him, but didn't know how to tell him…how to show him. God only knew she had the will—she just… She needed to find the way.

She watched, and listened, as he talked with the easy-going Barrett. Jealousy twisted through her insides as she heard the soldier mention the village. She might be an innocent when it came to the intimacies between a man and woman, but she wasn't a fool. She knew precisely what men went to the village for—and she would have bet everything she owned that Rhys had no trouble attracting female companionship when he was there, whether it was bought or given freely. No, attracting women would never be a problem for a man like him. He was the most darkly masculine, purely male, utterly seductive creature Alia had ever seen, and she was completely enthralled by him.

"Not that he's ever given you *any* reason to hope," she muttered under her breath. At nearly twenty-four, Alia knew she was already well past what was considered her prime. It had never bothered her until Rhys had arrived to oversee her father's protection, but now the knowledge burned like a physical pain within her chest. One she knew there was little she could do to ease. Despite the wonderful gifts she'd inherited from her mother, she had taken a vow to never abuse them, which meant that the brooding soldier would have to come to her of his own volition. She wouldn't compel him with potions or spells, no matter how tempting it was to think of drawing his notice. Something other than those hard, angry glares he always gave her, as if it was a crime for her to be anywhere near him.

With her heartache locked tight in her chest, she watched his retreating back until Mrs. Blackstone, their cottagekeeper, called her name from the kitchen and then she finally pushed away from the wall, heading indoors. Alia went through the next few hours lost in her daydreams, wondering how she was going to finally get the dark, brooding warrior to talk to her. Mrs. Blackstone headed home to her ailing husband, leaving Alia to serve dinner while she racked her brain for a way to draw Rhys's attention that wouldn't make her look like a pathetic fool. Though, truth be told, she was no longer worried about her pride. As far as Alia was concerned, her pride could be damned, if it meant finding a way to get close to the mysterious soldier.

The evening meal passed by in a blur, and afterward her father headed back to his study to continue with his research. She'd already secluded herself in her room for the evening, sitting on her window seat as she stared out at the harvest moon, lost in her thoughts, when her father's voice intruded into her mind.

Alia, you must listen! And whatever you do, do not try to come to my study!

With a gasp, her spine went straight as she stared sightlessly through the window, the urgency of her father's mental communication alerting her to the gravity of the situation. Though this was hardly the first time he'd communicated with her in such a manner, it was obvious from his tone that something was horribly wrong.

We've been betrayed by one of the Consortium guards. The rest of Rhys's men are dead, their bodies already destroyed. I haven't much time, and there's nothing to be done for me now. They have a seer with them—an old crone who's embraced the dark arts. I'll try to keep her from learning my secrets, but I don't know how long I'll be able to hold together. You must hurry! Go to the secret place, Alia. Take the cross that's hidden there.

He then sent her a torrent of images, the strange blend of mental pictures somehow explaining more than he had time to relay with words. They flashed through her mind with dizzying speed, one after another, and then faded away as her father softly said, *You must go, this instant. Then find Rhys as soon as you have the cross, Alia. I'm handing you over into his protection now. You can trust him, daughter. He'll watch over you. Always, I promise. And never forget that I love you....*

With a sob on her lips, she briefly considered disobeying his command and rushing to her father's rescue, but she could already feel his connection fading. He was leaving her, passing into the afterlife, and there was nothing she could do to stop it. Choking back her selfish heartache, she grabbed up the flickering candle that sat on her desk and made her way into the secret passage built into the paneled surface of her bedroom wall, quickly closing it behind her. The passageway was cool as she raced through the thick, candlelit darkness, the only sound that of her soft crying. It wasn't easy, but she forced herself to choke back the tears, painfully aware that they were not what her father would have wanted. She knew the tears were for her own sense of loss and the fact that she was going to miss him so desperately.

Though it would have been difficult for a human to understand, death was viewed differently by a Reavess and her mate—and even worked differently, without the pain and suffering that most species endured at the time of passing into their "next life" as the Reavess called it. Knowing he was going to die, not only would her father have been able to separate his spirit from the suffering of his mortal body, but her mother's spirit would have been waiting for him, the two soul mates finally reunited after years apart. So while it was a tragic event for Alia, she knew that it had been a joyous one for her father, who was now with the woman he loved—his other half. Her father had lost his wife much too young, and there was no doubt that the wait had been painful for him. As the soul mate of a Reavess, he'd had the power to cast off his mortal body at any time and join his beloved, as most Reavess did, the pain of being without their other half simply too difficult to bear. But he'd remained in this world for Alia's sake, not wanting her to be alone.

Now, as she felt his connection fade to black, she knew that he was where he was meant to be. Where he would finally be happy.

At the end of the passage, she came to a ladder that led to a small door in the floor of the greencottage. Moving as quickly as she could with only one free hand, Alia made her way up the ladder and through the opening, closed the trapdoor behind her, then blew out the candle and set it down, the moonlight just thick enough for her to make her way between the rows of flowers. She had just opened the door, stepping out into the cool air of the night, when a hand suddenly closed over her mouth and a hard, powerful body pressed close against her back. She panicked, sucking in a deep breath, and instantly recognized her captor's warm, rich scent as he pulled her into the shadowed edge of the forest.

"Don't be scared," he whispered, taking his hand away. "I'm not going to hurt you."

"Rhys?" she breathed out, turning to stare up at him as he took hold of her shoulders. The silvery moonlight cast the rugged angles of his face into sharp relief, highlighting the thick scar that slashed across his left temple. The grip of his large hands was strong enough to bruise, the tremor in his hard muscles hinting at just how difficult it was for him to control himself. To keep from hurting her? Out of anger? Or because he wanted to chase down the traitors and make them pay for what he'd done?

Before she could decide on an answer, she found herself hauled up against his hard body. "What—" she started to gasp, before he made a deep, predatory animal sound, cutting off her whispered exclamation with the hard, devastating heat of his mouth. Her heart nearly burst from her chest as he ravaged her with the bold, aggressive sweep of his tongue, tasting her deeply…thoroughly. Then he wrenched himself away, his breathing so harsh and violent that she could feel the warm heat of his breath against her face. He took a step back from her, and then another, as if he needed to put distance between them.

"What was that for?" she whispered, touching her fingertips to her tingling lips, wishing he would do it again…and again.

"Damn it, I didn't mean to do that." He made a thick sound in his throat that seemed equal parts hunger and rage, his body held hard and tight, as if he was fighting to hold himself in place. "I just… I thought you might already be dead when I got here and found there was no one guarding the cottage, and I *had* to know," he all but snarled, the guttural words making her shiver with awareness.

"Know what?"

His fingers flexed at his sides, and then he quickly fisted them into hard, tight knots. "What you taste like," he muttered, his glittering stare boring into her, as though he was trying to read her mind…to see her soul.

She blinked, undone as much by his words as she was by that devastating kiss. "And?"

"And what?" he grunted, that fierce, hungry gaze

dropping to her mouth, following the curve of her lower lip as she wet it with a quick swipe of her tongue.

"Wh-what do I taste like?" She swallowed, half terrified to know the answer as he seemed to force himself to look away from her, staring into the shadowed forest that surrounded them.

Alia didn't think he would answer, and then he finally spoke, his deep voice as dark and delicious as the rest of him . "Like a woman," he rasped, the deep-creased scowl he cut her from the corner of his eye no doubt meant to keep her quiet.

"Hmm." The hope in her stomach turned sour. "I suppose you've tasted so many of us, we all just…what? Taste the same now? One's as good as another?"

"What the hell are you talking about?" he snapped, looking as if he thought she'd lost her mind. In a way, it felt as if she had. As if the Alia she knew had been left behind on the window seat in her room, and now a stranger was standing in her place. One whose beloved father was gone. Whose life was now in mortal danger. And who'd just experienced her first kiss in the moon-drenched darkness, Rhys's mouthwatering taste still warm in her mouth, seductive and rich, moving through her veins like a hot, potent wine.

"Nothing," she mumbled, realizing that now was

hardly the time to get into an argument. But it was impossible not to feel the sharp burn of jealousy when she imagined just how many women had been gifted with his dark, breathtaking kisses.

"How did you get here?" he suddenly demanded, pinning her with his steely stare. "How did you get out of the cottage? I was just getting ready to search for you, when I saw you walking through the greencottage." His rough tone made it clear that he'd been terrified for her safety.

"I escaped through a secret passage that leads from my room to the greenhouse." At the slight widening of his eyes, she said, "Although my father might not be a warrior, he's always cunning. But what are *you* doing here? I thought you were in the village."

"I came back," he rasped, his rough-velvet voice stroking over her sensitive flesh like a caress as he held her stare, the smoldering look in his eyes making her wonder if he was lying about her taste. Maybe there *had* been something special about it—something that set her apart from all the other women he'd known. She wanted so badly to believe that, but took a shaky breath, fully aware that she was projecting her own desperate longing onto him, and at a most inopportune time.

He tore his gaze from hers again to glance at the

cottage that stood silent and still in the distance, then gave her a stern look of warning. "I need you to stay here while I go and check on your father."

She shook her head as she quietly said, "There's no need. He told me we were betrayed by one of your men, and that this man killed the other guards."

"Who was it?" he growled, looking as if he would explode with rage.

"I don't know," she replied, hating that she had to be the one to tell him of the betrayal and deaths. The other soldiers were his friends—men he'd trusted with his life. "His identity was concealed and my father couldn't tell which one it was. The traitor had others with him, but they've already left. My father made them think that I'd made a run for the village. That's where they've headed to search for me."

"What were they after?" he demanded with a fierce scowl, an unmistakable rage still burning in his eyes at the knowledge that one of his men had turned traitor. Alia knew he would want to go and find him, but they didn't have time.

"The same thing we're after." When he narrowed his eyes, she rushed to explain. "Just before I left the cottage, my father charged me with a mission. We have to get an ancient cross from its hiding place in the grotto, and then retrieve the others of its kind from a cave in Somerset as quickly as possible. His attackers tried to use a seer to learn where they're hidden, but he thinks he was able to keep the location of the cave concealed. No matter what, he said the traitor must not be allowed to get his hands on the crosses."

She could see the surprise in his eyes, the pale gray burning silver in the moonlight. "You talked with him?"

"Well, no, not exactly," she explained. "I was in my room, and the traitors already had him trapped in his study."

"Alia, you're not making any sense." His words were cut with a sharp edge of impatience. "If you weren't in the room with him, then how in God's name did he tell you anything?"

As she witnessed his confusion, the corner of her mouth twitched with a movement that couldn't quite make its way into a smile. "Because he spoke into my mind."

There was a strange silence for a moment, like something thick and heavy settling between them, and then he quietly said, "Are you telling me that your father can read your thoughts?"

"If he chose to. But he wouldn't invade my privacy that way."

Rhys looked a little green, and she frowned. "What is it?"

"Can he do it to anyone?" he rasped.

She stared at him for a moment in confusion, and then began to comprehend. "You're worried he would be angry about the things you've had in your mind, aren't you?"

"Angry? Nay, Alia. He would put his sword through me," he muttered in a low, resigned voice.

She raised her brows, a tiny shoot of hope blooming to life within her chest. "Do tell."

He glared, his mouth grim as he said, "Not for all the gold in the world. I have no desire to be castrated by a man reputed to be a scholar on all things medieval."

She would have laughed at the shudder that moved across his broad shoulders—would have gone light-headed at the mere suggestion that Rhys's thoughts might have been about her—but the heartbreaking thought of what she'd lost that night sobered her. "Well, you won't have to worry about that now." The words were quiet, thickened by the tears that burned in her throat. "He was already gone before I made it into the greenhouse."

"Wherever they've taken him," he vowed in a low voice, "we'll get him back."

She could see his determination to do just that carved into the fierce lines of his expression, and her mouth trembled with grief. "He isn't their prisoner, Rhys. The methods they used to try and invade his mind were too much, and he was forced to move on before they broke him."

A sharp, biting curse immediately fell from his lips. The foul word would have shocked her if she hadn't already heard it repeated time and again when she'd been spying on the guards during their training. Rhys studied her expression through shadowed eyes, no doubt looking for the soul-stricken grief expected from a daughter who'd been so obviously devoted to her father. In a low voice, he said, "I expected you to be…"

His words trailed off, and she shook her head again, looking away. "Devastated?" she asked. "Torn by inconsolable grief?"

"Yes," he said simply.

She firmed her jaw, forcing herself to meet his stare. "There's a part of me inside that's selfish enough to be heartbroken that he's gone, but I refuse to give into it. Not when I know how happy he is to finally be reunited with my mother. He only stayed behind because of me.

Now that he's handed me into your care, he felt free to go on, where he's wanted to be since the moment we lost her."

A new tension swept over his large body, and though he wasn't touching her, she could feel it blasting against her, nearly knocking her backward with its force. "What do you mean he handed you into my care?" His voice was soft, but harsh. "I don't understand."

She managed a tear-filled grin as she caught the flare of panic in his eyes. "The last words he said to me were that you would be my protector now."

"Till we get these bloody crosses," he countered in a rough voice, and she couldn't miss the thick edge of dread in his graveled words.

The grin somehow found the strength to bloom into a wry, shaky smile, and Alia quietly said, "Nay, Rhys. Believe it or not, he honestly meant forever."

3

If he made it through the night without expiring from lust, Rhys knew it would be a miracle. A pathetic truth, but one that was painfully correct. He was filled with rage for the loss of his friends. With hatred for the one who had betrayed them. And then there was the guilt for his failure to protect Matthew Buchanan, a man he'd not only respected, but had genuinely liked. A man who had always treated Rhys as an intellectual equal, instead of the mindless soldier that so many assumed him to be. Rage, hatred, guilt… Each of the violent, twisting emotions seethed through his insides, painful and strong—and yet they could not eclipse his searing, growing need for one delicate little female.

Whatever you do, you must be strong. You can't give in. Can't allow even a moment of weakness.

Standing at the mouth of the cave he'd found buried in the side of a rocky cliff, Rhys silently muttered the words of warning to himself again and again as he stared out over the stygian forest that spread for miles below them. There was complete stillness in the night, not even a rustling wind in the trees to break the silence, as if the fog-drenched darkness had swallowed all sound. The misty vapor twined around the nearby trees like slithering serpents, giving the sense that the night itself was something to be feared. As if it held untold dangers and deadly secrets.

And yet it wasn't the unknown danger in the night that frightened him. No, his greatest threat was already there. So close, his heightened senses could hear the soft rasp of her breath…the sensual pounding of her heart.

Behind him, Alia sat beside the small fire he'd started, no doubt trying to warm her frigid body. She deserved a soft bed for the night, but they were traveling the most direct route to the mysterious Wookey Hole Caves in Somerset where the crosses were hidden, and there'd been nowhere else for them to stop.

It'd taken only moments to find the beautiful cross her

father had hidden in the grotto not far from her cottage, and after Rhys had retrieved his horse from the stable, they'd immediately been on their way. Unfortunately, the night turned brutally cold for their journey, chilling Alia to the bone. Though she hadn't once complained, he'd heard her teeth chattering during the last few hours of their ride, her slender form shivering violently against the front of his body, where he'd perched her atop his stallion.

Rhys had longed to wrap his arms around her, drawing her closer against him, but hadn't dared. His restraint had already been worn thin just from being close to her, her tender scent filling his head...drawing the predator in him closer and closer to the surface. He'd wanted to get her as far from the Buchanan cottage as possible before they stopped, but was afraid of pushing her too hard, and so they'd finally taken shelter in the cave. And while it was quiet and peaceful, Rhys knew that he would find no rest within the damp hollow.

He honestly meant forever....

Her strange words kept working their way through his mind, too shocking to fully comprehend. Her father must have gone mad. That was the only explanation Rhys could think of for Matthew Buchanan's outlandish declaration.

As if sensing his internal thoughts, Alia's soft voice suddenly drifted to his ears. "I'm sorry that you found my father's words so upsetting. I, um, I certainly don't plan to hold you to them."

He turned, bracing his shoulder against the rocky wall as he met her gaze. "I just can't figure out what the hell he was thinking. You must have misunderstood him."

She wrapped her arms around her knees, looking away to stare into the dancing flames of the fire. "Honestly, Rhys, I was only teasing when I told you. There's no reason to keep brooding."

"Then he didn't say that?" he demanded, feeling as if she'd just ripped the floor out from under him. "You *lied* to me?"

"No, I didn't lie. That *is* what he told me," she said huskily, biting the corner of her lower lip. "But then my father was always a hopeless romantic. It seems he had some fanciful notion in his head that you secretly care for me, and that we would stay together. I just... I know that it's impossible. I didn't mean to upset you, and I have no intention of making myself a nuisance by following after you. Obviously, you're free to do as you like."

He grunted at that, and began pacing from one side of the small cave to the other, the coiled tension in his body no doubt visible in every hard, muscular line, radiating a hot, violent blast of aggression. She should have been terrified at the thought of being alone with him, but for some reason, she seemed to feel perfectly safe there in his presence.

"Will someone bury him?" she asked softly, the small catch in her voice reminding him that she was inwardly grieving, no matter how brave a face she tried to put on for him. He wanted to go to her and wrap her up in his arms, cradling her against his chest, and offer what comfort he could, but knew it was too dangerous. It had been bad enough having her so close as they'd ridden, when his mind was focused on making sure they weren't being followed. Now that they had settled in for the night, with no distractions, it was imperative that he keep as much distance between them as he could.

And yet he seemed to keep moving closer…and closer.

Clearing his throat, he answered her question, saying, "I'm sure Mrs. Blackstone will return to the cottage tomorrow. When she discovers what's happened, she'll see to it that his body is cared for. But you mustn't go back there, Alia. *Ever.* There's no telling who's after these crosses, and no way of knowing how many others they're working with. Finding them is only going to solve the first problem. After that, we've got to figure out what to do with them."

And then he would have to figure out what to do with *her.*

She nodded, her small body rocking back and forth, as if she were trying to keep warm...or seek comfort from the rhythmic motion. God only knew she'd been through hell that night, only to be stuck there with him. Though Rhys knew he should have been feeling rank and vile after everything that had happened, just watching her seemed to gentle his icy anger, her alluring scent teasing his nose...his senses. It was that familiar, provocative scent of heated jasmine that he associated with Alia, and he wondered how she always managed to smell so delicious. Was it in her soap? Or did she rub the flower's oil into her naked flesh, so that the evocative scent rose with the heat of her body, with each heavy pulse of her heart?

Desperate to steer his mind into safer territory, he pushed a few windblown strands of hair back from his forehead and said, "Tell me about your father's work." She'd briefly explained during the ride about the images her father had put into her mind, the montage relaying what they needed to do, but Rhys had several questions that he wanted answered.

She hugged her legs tighter against her body, still gently rocking, a deep breath shuddering from her lungs as she turned her head to meet his gaze. "Well, you already know about his studies—his secret search for the lost archives. Somehow they led him to the ancient caves in Wookey Hole. Not knowing for sure what the crosses were or why they'd been hidden there, he took only one, intending to study it. He was hoping it might lead to the archives, but it didn't."

"Did he have any idea why anyone would want them?" he asked. "Any theories on their purpose?"

She nodded her head slowly. "My father had his suspicions."

He arched his brows, waiting for her to continue. She seemed to take a moment to collect her thoughts, then said, "Have you ever heard of the Dark Markers?"

"The weapons meant to destroy the Casus?" he asked with a note of surprise, remembering the stories he'd first heard as a child. The Casus were a sadistic, mutated clan who had gone to war with the Merrick hundreds of years ago—the conflict lasting until the Consortium had finally imprisoned the Casus in an unknown holding ground, where the immortal monsters were no doubt still rotting away. The Casus's indiscriminate killing of human victims had brought about the rise of the Collective

Army, which had destroyed the first Consortium. Rumor had it that before their destruction, the Consortium had managed to create weapons—the Dark Markers—that would actually destroy a Casus's soul, their intention to return to the hidden holding ground and execute the vile race once and for all. But when the members of the Consortium had been killed, the archives had been lost, along with any record of the Markers, as well as the location of the holding ground itself. For centuries, those who knew about the Consortium's plans had speculated about whether the Markers had ever even actually been created, or if they were merely nothing more than folklore.

She nodded again in answer to his question, while the dancing firelight brought out the reddish tones in the long hair streaming over her graceful shoulders, down the graceful line of her back. "There's been endless speculation about what the Dark Markers looked like, but my father believed that the crosses he'd found might actually be them. If he was right, who do you think would want the weapons enough to kill for them?"

His fury roiled at the thought of one of his friends turning traitor, but he beat it down. Better to think about it later, when Alia wasn't there to be harmed if he lost control. Trying to get a grip on his rage, he said,

"I'm not sure, but I suppose it could be the Collective. I know they've been as desperate to reach the archives as the Consortium has been. But I'm not sure what the Collective would want with the Markers. I mean, unless they knew how to use them to get into the holding ground and kill the Casus. But you'd think they'd come after clansmen like us before worrying about the ones who are locked away."

"My father thought there was another purpose," she told him. "One that the original Consortium had probably written about in the archives. One that would be a dangerous threat if it ended up in the wrong hands. It could be that someone out there knows this. Someone who would want to help the Casus in some way."

He swore under his breath at the thought, then glanced toward the beautiful cross that rested against her chest, the firelight glittering against its metallic surface. "May I see it?" he asked.

She took the cross from where it hung around her neck on a velvet cord and offered it up to him as he approached, saying, "It's very beautiful. And warm. I swear you can feel its power thrumming beneath its surface."

Taking it from her hand, Rhys crouched down beside the crackling fire and studied the strange object, wondering if it could truly be one of the legendary Markers. It was in the shape of a Maltese cross, with four thick, equal arms, the surface covered in tiny, intricate symbols that he didn't recognize. Fashioned from a black, glossy metal, it should have been cold to the touch, but was actually warm, just as she'd said, burning against his skin, as well as heavier than he'd expected. Rhys did his best to keep his attention focused on his study of the cross, searching his mind for where he might have seen the symbols before, but Alia's presence was too distracting. Her scent was stronger now, her skin warmed by the fire, making it difficult for him to think beyond how badly he wanted to touch her…taste her. He knew the danger he was courting in allowing his thoughts to drift into such treacherous territory, but he couldn't stop.

"Whoever wants them must be powerful. Powerful enough to find my father and turn one of your men." She pulled in a soft, trembling breath, then slowly let it out. "That means they're powerful enough to kill us, as well."

The change in topic jarred him, and he almost gave a deep, throaty laugh, only just managing to choke off the uncharacteristic sound at the last moment. Here he'd been wondering how she managed to smell so mouthwateringly good, and she sat beside him, worrying over whether she was going to live or die.

Lust, it seemed, had finally addled his brain.

"No one will get near you, Alia. Not if I can help it," he said in a low voice, handing the cross back to her, careful to avoid the touch of her fingers.

"But they're going to try to kill us, aren't they?" she asked, setting the cross beside her on the blanket, before looking back at him.

A sharp, bitter sound scraped his throat. "Killing wouldn't be the first thing they'd do to you," he said quietly.

For a moment, she appeared uncertain of his meaning, and then she gave a slow nod of understanding. "You're right. They'll want me to tell them everything that my father might have shared with me. They'll want to know what I know.."

"Among other things," he muttered under his breath.

Her head tilted the barest fraction to the side, her look quizzical, as if she didn't understand, and he heard himself saying, "My men could never take their eyes off you, Barrett included. You bewitch every man who sees you."

She made a shy sound of embarrassment and rolled her eyes. "That's ridiculous."

"It's not," he said in such a low voice, he doubted she'd even heard him.

It was a moment before she said anything more. Instead, she simply watched him, her dark eyes studying him through her long lashes, as if she were trying to see beneath his skin. Inside his head. Beneath his shields. It made him feel…odd. He would have thought the strange feeling was nervousness, but he'd never been nervous about anything in his life. To be nervous, you had to care. And he'd never really cared much about anything, either, except for his friends…the safety of those under his protection.

And this one mesmerizing witch.

Finally, her gaze slid away, focusing on the cave wall as she said, "Well, I never would have noticed their attention. I was always—" she looked down, gave a soft, nervous laugh "—I was always too busy watching *you.*"

"Alia." Her name fell from his lips like a hard, biting scrape of sound.

"Yes?" The word was nothing more than a barely there whisper, her eyes still not meeting his, her pale fingers wound together in a tense, clenching knot.

"Don't," he warned her, his voice so thick and rough, it barely sounded human.

She took another deep breath, then slowly lifted her face, her shy, luminous gaze finding his, staring straight into him. The look there was so tender and bright that he almost flinched. "Don't what?"

"Play games with me," he said with a hard bite of warning. "You'll find yourself... It could be... Just *don't*."

"I wasn't playing a game," she whispered. "I was just trying to be honest, Rhys. There's been so much silence between us, I thought it might be nice to speak the truth for once."

He rolled his shoulder, his body going hot more from the look in her deep blue eyes than the heat of the fire. "You were wrong," he said flatly.

"You'd rather I lie?" she asked, raising her brows.

He closed his eyes, silently begging for patience, wondering why she'd decided to torture him this way. Was she in shock? Or simply bored? In need of a distraction? Whatever the reason, it was going to destroy him.

"No," he finally forced out, his tone grim. "I don't want you to lie. Just...keep your words to yourself. The silence between us is a good thing. Trust me."

"Well, I refuse to sit here in silence with nothing but my thoughts for company," she said tightly, clearly frustrated with him. "So it seems you'll have to talk to me, after all."

Lifting his lashes, he sent her a cautious look. "What exactly do you wish to talk about?"

"Well, you could tell me about your life."

"What about it?" he asked warily. "You already know I'm a soldier. There isn't much else to it than that."

"Of course there is," she said with the natural streak of persistence that set her so far apart from the other young women he'd known. Most girls Alia's age were raised to be demure, soft-spoken creatures who were skittish around men. And while she was no doubt gentle, she had been brought up by a father who'd adamantly believed in the equality of the sexes. As a result, the young Reavess was not only a powerful witch, but she was also well-educated and had been encouraged to speak her mind from an early age.

For instance, she went on to say, holding his gaze, "what is our home like? How long have you been a soldier? How old are you? What are your parents like? Do you see them often?"

A ragged thread of humorless laughter rumbled up from his chest, and he almost smiled, thinking that she'd found a way to momentarily cool his ardor without even trying. If ever there was a topic to turn him cold, it was the couple who'd sired him. "My home is wherever the Consortium sends me. I've been a soldier since I was fifteen… I'm now twenty-eight. And I haven't had anything to do with my parents in years."

"Really? Why not?"

He could have simply told her the matter was none of her business, but for some reason he couldn't seem to get the words out. Instead, he said, "Because that's how they prefer it."

"I could do the gentlemanly thing and keep from prying, but my parents always said that I was too curious for my own good. And in case you didn't notice, I'm not a gentleman," she added wryly, the heat of her gaze pressing in on him, making his skin go slick beneath his clothes…making his blood go thick. "So I'm going to be rude and pry. In fact, I'm going to demand an explanation."

Rhys watched her intently from the corner of his eye, simply not knowing what to make of her. Any other young woman in her position would have been huddled against the far wall in fear, but not Alia. Instead, she sat there on the hard floor of the cave with only a thin blanket from his saddle roll to soften the ground beneath her,

her delicate chin propped atop her bent knees, staring at him with bright eyes, while a small smile seemed to be hiding at the corner of her mouth, teasing him with its presence.

Feeling as if he'd entered a dream state, Rhys suddenly heard himself telling her the story of how his mother, who had hated the dragon clans, had been forced into wedding his father, the heir to one of the most powerful Charteris families that remained in existence. Her father had been a nobleman from one of the dormant ancient bloodlines who'd wanted to infuse some fresh, powerful blood within his family, giving his daughter no choice in her future.

From the moment they'd said their vows, his parents had been at war. His mother had often said that bedding a Charteris was something that only a whore could enjoy, claiming they were the most savage, primitive creatures she'd ever encountered. She'd endured until she'd become pregnant, providing his father with his heir, and then she'd banned him from her bed.

When it became clear that Rhys couldn't fully take the shape of the Charteris's beloved beast, his father had eventually left, wanting nothing more to do with either of them ever again. Rhys had always been surprised that his father simply hadn't killed them both. It had been in his ability to do so, even in his nature. And in a way, it might have been kinder. Being left behind with his mother had been a sort of death in itself, as she'd done her best to make the son pay each day for the sins of the men she'd claimed had ruined her life.

"Why did your father agree to marry her?" Alia asked, when he'd finished giving her the bare bones of the story.

"I don't know," he admitted in a quiet rasp, rolling his shoulder. "I'm sure he had his reasons, but I never knew what they were. It's a miracle that he avoided killing her in their marriage bed, but then he was reported to have amazing control over his beast."

"How would he have killed her?" she asked, a small vee settling between her slender brows at the thought.

Rhys ground his jaw, wondering why he couldn't just keep his mouth shut around her. "They fought a lot," he muttered, reaching over to the pile of small branches he'd collected and tossing another one onto the fire, his tone warning her that it was all the explanation he would give.

"And where did the scars come from?" she asked, her tone exquisitely gentle. "The ones I've seen on your back."

"My father," he replied, working to keep his voice

even, instead of snarling the words. "Since he couldn't get me to willingly shift, he thought he could beat the beast out of me. But I was too stubborn."

"What do you mean?"

He stared into the flames as he explained. "I think I could have probably completed a full shift, or close to it, as I got older, but I refused to allow it to happen, burying that part of me deep inside, where he couldn't reach it. I...I didn't want to be like him, and so I used everything I had to fight it down."

She couldn't even begin to hide her horror as she quietly said, "That must have been incredibly difficult."

Rhys shook his head. "I've done it for so long now, I don't even know if I could call the traits forward if I needed to."

"But it must be hard," she murmured, "always fighting that part of yourself."

He shrugged, saying, "It's like second nature now."

The words were true, and yet Rhys knew his actions weren't without consequence. The longer he fought what he was, the colder he became, until it felt as if a hard, thick casing of ice had hardened around his heart. One that had been slowly squeezing the organ to death, until the first time he'd felt the breathtaking warmth of Alia's smile...and the ice had begun to splinter.

"And your mother never did anything to stop him?"

He couldn't help but laugh. "No," he said around the dark edges of sound. "She didn't stop him."

"I'm sorry they were both so horrible," she said after a moment, an unmistakable note of sincerity in her husky voice. "It seems so unfair that I had two wonderful parents, and you didn't even have one."

Rhys felt himself go hot around the ears, realizing how pathetic his upbringing must have sounded to someone like Alia, whose father had clearly adored her. "Don't feel sorry for me. I didn't need them to care about me, so no harm was done."

She gave him a look that made him inwardly cringe, as if she'd seen beneath his roughly spoken words, to the stark, embarrassing truth. The one he refused to admit even to himself. Finally, she looked away, staring once again into the flickering, golden flames of the fire. She was silent for the moment, thinking about God only knew what. The look in her big, endlessly blue eyes was distant, making it impossible for him to guess her thoughts. Just as he was getting ready to demand to know what she was thinking, she said, "I've always sensed an internal conflict within you, Rhys, and now I understand what it is. You fight what you are, because of your father. You need to stop resisting and learn to embrace your true nature, if you're ever going to find the peace and happiness that you deserve."

"And how would you know what I need?" he drawled, a cynical bite to his words that he hoped would keep her quiet, before he ended up making a complete fool of himself. "You're little more than a child."

Her chin lifted in a mulish expression that would have made him smile, if not for the fact that he was using every ounce of strength and will he had not to touch her. Not to take her beneath his hands, beneath his body, and thrust himself so deep within her, she'd be marked forever by the memory of his possession.

Only, it would be too short a memory, considering he would end up taking her life.

He ground his jaw so hard he was surprised his teeth didn't crack, and watched the color bloom in her cheeks as she said, "I'm nearly twenty, Rhys. Hardly a child."

He gave a tired sigh. "You're still too young, Alia. And far too innocent to be here like this with me. I don't know what the hell your father was thinking."

"Humph," she mumbled under her breath, obviously annoyed with him. He started to rise, thinking she'd remain blessedly silent now, but then she said, "One last question, and then I'll leave you in peace."

He stood before the fire, staring down at her, wondering what it was going to take to make her leave him alone, before he did something they would both regret.

"What's your last name?" she asked, her head tilted back so that she could see his eyes.

"I don't have one," he said, relieved that this, at least, had been a simple one.

That small crease nestled between her brows again. "How can you not have a last name?"

"Easily," he replied dryly. "My father's family name was MacInnes, but he refused to share it with me until it'd been determined if I could fully shift—which I never did. So I've gone by Rhys my entire life."

"You know, I hate to speak ill of people I've never met," she muttered, her mouth pressed into a thin line, "but I'm afraid I don't care for your parents, Rhys. They sound like complete bastards."

A low, rough-edged rumble of laughter vibrated up from his chest, and he looked away, staring back out into the foggy night through the mouth of the cave. Without looking her way, he finally said, "You should get some sleep, Alia. Tomorrow is going to be a long day if we're to make Wookey Hole by nightfall."

"Are you going to rest as well?" she asked, and he looked down in time to see the slight shiver that trembled across her slender shoulders beneath the dark blue of her dress. And suddenly, from one heartbeat to the next, he had a dangerous vision of his big hands undoing the tiny buttons that closed the dress's fitted bodice...of him peeling back that blue fabric to reveal the pale, intimate beauty beneath. He could see himself pressing his open mouth against the urgent beating of her heart. Could see himself turning his head and hungrily taking her perfect, delicate breast into his mouth...touching it with his tongue, while his hand pushed its way demandingly between her slender thighs.

His body instantly went rock hard at the sweet, erotic image, his cock thickening beneath the buttons of his trousers. Cursing roughly under his breath, he tore his gaze from her body, working to keep his breathing quiet and even, thankful that his shirt hung down to cover his erection. After a moment, he was able to say, "I'll sleep eventually." Being careful not to look in her direction, he bent down again to quickly throw another piece of wood on the fire, worried that she would grow cold. "But I want to keep an eye on things for a while longer."

4

As the small branch smoldered within the flames, Rhys started to move back to his feet, and Alia realized that she was letting him get away without even trying to keep him near. Without even making an effort to keep him close. Choking down the cold fear of rejection that had lodged in her throat, she suddenly moved to her knees, took hold of his strong neck and pulled him down to her. She wanted to taste his delicious mouth once again, losing herself in its warmth, its heat.

He made a thick sound of surprise, his hands curling around her arms, his corded throat hot beneath her chilled palms. *Don't push me away*, she thought desperately, pressing her mouth harder to his, hoping to hold him with her kiss. His body had gone rigid with shock, his pulse throbbing violently beneath her hands, but he didn't pull back…didn't shove her away. Praying that she could seduce him, Alia touched her tongue to his warm lips, her heart beating like a frightened, excited bird within her chest. He gave a low growl that was savagely hot against her mouth, and then he exploded into movement, taking control of the kiss…of *her*. Suddenly she was lying against the thin blanket, Rhys's hard, muscular body covering her, holding her down, while he claimed her mouth with a dark, devastating skill that made her want to scream with need. Made her want to seek relief for the hot, heavy ache that had settled within her, pulsing through her body. She needed his weight against her. Needed his touch…his possession.

"Oh, God, Rhys," she gasped as he broke the kiss, his bent legs straddling her hips while his hands moved to the bodice of her gown. She gripped handfuls of his thick, silken hair as he pressed a string of damp kisses down the curve of her throat, his fingers working to undo the tiny row of buttons. Just when she was sure he was at the end of his patience and would rip the garment open, he pushed both the loosened bodice and crinkled chemise beneath her breasts, baring them to his blistering gaze.

"Christ, Alia." His voice was ragged, harsh, the look

in his eyes scorching as he stared down at her chest. He slowly dragged his gaze higher, over the delicate line of her collarbone, up to her heavy-lidded eyes, then back down again, until he was staring hungrily at her right breast, his callused thumb rubbing over the pale outer curve again and again. His breathing became harder... louder, as if he were struggling to take in each deep, soughing pull of air. "You're so soft," he rasped, his voice so low she could barely hear the words.

An expression of awe—of pure, primal hunger and need—darkened his beautiful face, and then he lowered his head until she could feel the smoldering warmth of his breath against her cool skin. He nuzzled the delicate curves with his nose...and then he licked her, while a deep, rumbling growl vibrated against her sensitive flesh. The smooth, velvety stroke of his tongue moved along the inner swell of her breast, and then he did it again, slowly working his way around the swollen, hardened tip, her nipple aching with the need to feel that warm, delicious heat surrounding it...pulling on it. She arched beneath him, feeling burned.

"Rhys," she cried breathlessly, laying her hands on the back of his neck, loving the strength she could feel beneath his hot, silky skin. "You're so beautiful...so warm."

He stiffened, as if her words had in some way alarmed him, and immediately started to pull away. "Don't," she groaned, refusing to release her hold on him, her fingers digging into his broad, muscular shoulders. "Please, Rhys. Don't pull away from me."

He closed his eyes, his face pulled into a tight, brutal expression of strain. "This is wrong, Alia."

"It can't be," she argued, her voice so husky she didn't even recognize it as her own. She knew there were things she had to tell him, confessions that would have to be made, but she *had* to find a way to get through to him first. Had to break her way through the emotional layers of armor that encased him if there was any chance of him opening his heart to her. It was insanity to hope that he actually cared, but she couldn't help it. It no longer mattered if she made a fool of herself. All that mattered was this dark, lonely, remarkable man who had shown her what it was to truly desire someone with every fiber of her being...to need him like she needed water and air—and had so easily stolen her heart. "I need you too badly for it to be wrong."

"No!" Wiping his mouth with the back of his wrist, he wrenched himself out of her hold, straightening on the knees that still straddled her hips, the muscles in his arms and thighs bulging against his dark clothing. His chest expanded with each of his rough, heavy breaths, while the horrified look on his face tore at her heart. He'd opened his eyes to reveal chips of cold, flinty gray, staring down at her as if he'd just discovered he'd been lying with a poisonous viper. Something deadly and cold that could destroy him if he got too close.

"Rhys?" she whispered, covering her bared chest with her trembling arms.

"I…can't," he forced out from behind his clenched teeth. "I can't get this close to you."

"What?" She shook her head, trying to understand.

He looked away, raking both hands back through his hair. "Damn it," he growled. His chilling gaze cut back to her face, and he narrowed his eyes, his voice thick with accusation as he said, "What the hell are you after?"

She blinked, feeling sick inside. The lines of suspicion on his dark face deepened, a strange, silvery glow in his eyes, as if a torrent of emotion was rioting through him. Unwilling to give up, she reached out to him with one hand, but he jerked away, moving swiftly to his feet. "Rhys, please," she called after him, lifting into a sitting position. "Please don't run from me. Just talk to me. Tell me what's wrong!"

Doing everything he could to fight her pull, Rhys

stepped away from her, breathing harshly from the effort of denying himself the one thing he hungered for with every cell of his body—and the one thing he could so easily destroy. "Christ, Alia. You have no idea what you're doing."

She hugged her arms around her body, her eyes glassy and bright, as if she was fighting back tears. "I just wanted to be close to you. To give you pleasure. But I got lost in the moment and was taking it all for myself, wasn't I?"

"For the love of…" His voice trailed away, and he swallowed, unable to believe he'd heard her correctly.

She took a deep breath, her expression determined as she said, "But if you'll just come back to me, I'll do my best to make you feel good, too."

A violent tremor shuddered its way through his body, and he took another step back, needing the distance, needing to be anywhere in the world but *there*, with her staring up at him like an exquisite virgin sacrifice, ready to offer herself up to his lust. Her draw was irresistible—warm and seductive and pure—calling to him like a siren, drugging his body and his mind. Compelling his very soul. And yet he had to find some way to fight it…to turn away from her.

She licked her lower lip, her eyes heavy with passion,

cheeks flushed, mouth swollen and red. He knew it would have been impossible to find a more desirable woman, no matter how intently he searched—just as he knew that she had no idea how badly he wanted her. How much he craved her, needed her.

"I know I have no experience, but I can be taught, Rhys. Surely you could tell me what I need to know to make you feel good."

He fisted his hands at his sides and his body shuddered, his muscles coiled, the hunger in his veins unlike anything he'd ever known. "For the love of all things holy, Alia. Please, just be quiet."

Her chin trembled, but she lifted it at a defiant angle. "Is it because you went to the village? Have you already had a woman tonight, then?"

"No," he growled for the second time. "I…I went to the tavern, but I wasn't…with anyone." He should have lied, but for some reason the truth was torn from his lips, and he could see the relief that brightened her eyes.

"I'm glad," she whispered. "I hated the thought of you going to another woman. I wanted…I wanted you to come to me."

Rhys covered his eyes with one hand, feeling as if he was on the verge of some great, horrifying emotion. Some dangerous, irrevocable sin, and he was terrified that he wouldn't have the strength to do the right thing.

"Please, don't say anything more," he rasped. "I can't take it."

"But—"

"No," he snarled, cutting her off. "No more!"

Without looking at her again, he turned away, and before she could say another word, Rhys stalked from the cave, taking refuge in the cold, quiet stillness of the night.

5

With a soft gasp on her lips, Alia opened her eyes to the breathtaking sight of Rhys crouched down beside her, his steely gaze focused intently on her face, as if he'd been staring at her while she slept. The heat was back in his eyes, scorching and bright, the silver more blinding than the early morning sun, making her blush.

"I wouldn't wake you so early," he said gruffly, taking his large, warm hand from her shoulder, "but we don't have any time to waste if we want to make Somerset by nightfall."

She cast a quick glance around the cave, pushing her tangled hair back from her brow as she looked for his bedding. "Didn't you sleep?" she asked, hoping her face didn't look as hot as it felt. Heat bloomed in her cheeks as she thought of what she'd done last night, throwing herself at him so shamelessly.

"A little," he murmured, not quite meeting her eyes, and she knew he was lying.

Taking a deep breath, Alia prepared to give voice to the words that needed to be said—words she'd put together as she'd lain on the thin blanket in the night, watching the dancing flames of the fire, waiting for him to return—before they set out on their journey. But as she stared at his ruggedly beautiful face, the sweet, piercing rush of desire scrambled her wits, her thoughts dissolving like sugar on her tongue. Shaking her head as she shifted into a sitting position, she cleared her throat and reached for the cross that lay on the blanket beside her. "Before we go," she murmured, the heat in her face growing warmer, "I need to talk to you."

"What is it?" he asked stiffly, clearly dreading whatever she had to say.

"This doesn't have to be your fight, Rhys. You can save yourself. Take this Marker," she said, offering it to him, "and trade it for your life if they come after you. I'll manage to get the others on my own."

"Is that right?" he asked quietly. She tried to read the look in his expressive eyes, but they were too narrow now, shadowed by the thick, heavy fringe of his lashes.

Alia nodded in response to his question, her breath held tight in her chest.

"Is that what you really think of me?" he said after a painful span of seconds, and there was something awful about his soft, quiet tone that made her flinch. "That I'd trade your life for my own? Leave you unprotected, while I run away with the cross?"

Her brow creased, the corners of her mouth tightening with a frown. "I'm not trying to insult you. I just don't see why you should endanger your life for someone who—" she lifted her shoulders in a tense shrug "—well, for someone who is merely a job to you. And I can manage well enough without you if I have to, Rhys. You needn't sacrifice yourself on my account."

He still crouched on the floor beside her, one arm resting on his bent knee, his other knee braced against the stone floor of the cave. His right hand rested on his hard thigh, and she watched as it tightened into a powerful fist, thick veins bulging beneath his dark skin. The fist shook with a slight tremor, as if he was fighting for control. "I apologize if I gave you the wrong impression last night, but I'm not going to leave you." His voice lowered, rough with emotion. "I would rather die, Alia, than leave you on your own."

"Don't say that!" she gasped, hating how comfortable

he seemed with the idea, as if his death would be nothing of consequence.

"I'm not afraid of dying." He took a deep breath, then slowly let it out. "The only thing that truly frightens me," he said, his eyes tight...dark, "is knowing that you're in danger. I have no intention of leaving your side until we've accomplished what we've set out to do and your life is no longer in jeopardy."

It sounded as if he was trying to choose his words with care, only to have them torn out against his will, revealing truths he would have rather kept locked away. Hidden from sight. Buried beneath his defenses.

"Then kiss me again," she suddenly heard herself say, the breathless words tumbling from her lips, unstoppable and soft. They were proof that she had no more control than he did, but then that was hardly surprising. The Reavess were known to be passionate creatures, often following their hearts against the dictates of their minds.

His eyes, which had been narrowed in insult, went wide with surprise. He didn't say anything right away, staring back at her with a thousand different emotions burning through those beautiful eyes, the mesmerizing color like a raging, thrashing sea of silver-tipped waves. She had no doubt that she'd shocked him with her direct manner, but she couldn't let that stop her. If she didn't push him, fighting against his resistance, then she was never going to reach him—never going to break her way through to the man hidden within.

"Please, Rhys." She reached out to touch his fisted hand, and saw the way he stiffened, as if he wasn't used to being touched. Not with kindness. And never with love. It broke her heart to think of his cold childhood. To think of all that he'd suffered. Curling her fingers around his hand, she said, "Just a kiss. Just one. And then I promise I'll leave you alone."

She was so sure he would refuse her that her heart almost burst with joy when he leaned close, her face suddenly held in the warm, strong hold of his hands, his mouth brushing against hers like a breathtaking, pleasure-drenched promise.

"Alia." That voice… God. So deep and dark and delicious. It was hypnotic. A low, rich rumble. Compelling… intoxicating with its beauty. The sound of that deep baritone saying her name was nearly her undoing. "Oh, Jesus. I tried to warn you last night that you shouldn't tempt me like this. It's so wrong, Alia."

Wrong? How could anything this wonderful possibly be wrong? she thought hazily, as he lowered her to the blanket, covering her with his hardness and his heat. "It doesn't feel wrong," she whispered, reaching up with her hand to touch the scratchy surface of his jaw. "It feels too good to be wrong, Rhys. It feels too good to stop."

"I'll no doubt go to hell for this, but if…if you trust me," he said huskily, touching his tongue to the beat of her pulse fluttering at the base of her throat, "I can give you more. But we have to be careful."

She answered eagerly with her body, spreading her legs beneath him as she arched her hips, and he growled, "Pull up your dress. Show me yourself, Alia."

His suddenly straightened arms shook as he lowered his gaze, watching as she gripped handfuls of crinkled blue fabric, slowly pulling her dress up, each grasping clutch revealing more…and more to his sharp, predatory gaze. Ankles and calves. Her bent knees and the pale inner surface of her thighs. She was endlessly thankful that she'd stripped her drawers off before going to sleep, leaving her naked beneath the dress.

As he stared down at her, his eyes burned. Smoldered. He made a rough sound deep in his throat, and then he was shifting position, his left arm bending, taking his weight as he pushed his right hand between her legs, palming the damp, tender flesh there. She cried out, shocked by the burst of sweet, wicked sensation that slammed through her, seizing her in a dizzying clutch of pleasure. Cursing an erotic string of words under his breath, he slipped his fingers knowingly through the drenched, intimate folds of her sex, while gazing down at her with a dark, powerful intensity, as if it would hurt him to look away. There was something painfully intimate about the look on his face as he touched that most sensitive part of her, and she trembled as his thumb stroked over the hardened knot of flesh that seemed to hold her heartbeat.

"Have you ever given yourself a release?" he asked, his voice low and rough. He stared into her eyes as he waited for her answer, and stroked the tip of his longest finger around her tender opening, again and again, until she was shaking and hot, her face damp. "Have you, Alia?"

She shook her head, sinking her teeth into her lower lip, knowing exactly what she wanted from him, despite her innocence. "Please," she whispered, arching, feeling as if she'd burn alive if he didn't help her… easing the heavy ache that had settled low in her body. As she pleaded, his eyes narrowed, crinkling sexily at the corners, and then he was sinking that long finger into her sex, pressing it inside…sinking deep, and she whimpered at the delicious sensation. "Oh, God," she said brokenly, lifting her hips, marveling at how different the penetration felt from anything she'd ever imagined. Her fantasies about him had always been soft-focused and sweet, like a girl's dreams. But Rhys touched her as though she was a woman, pulling that long, hot finger out to the mouth of her sex, then thrusting back in, working against the tight, natural resistance of her body.

"Lift your knees higher," he said in a raw voice, and as she followed his command, he worked a second finger in alongside the first, stretching that narrow part of her. Her skin was fever-damp and hot, as if heat were pouring from his hand, up into her body, melting her from the inside out. He thrust his fingers harder, deeper, the muscles bulging in his arm...his thumb rubbing wickedly against her softly pulsing clit. Leaning down, he scraped his teeth across her cloth-covered nipple, and she sobbed something that sounded too shivery to be pain. The breathtaking wave of pleasure grew, sensation building upon sensation like the spiraling, hypnotic notes of a song, and Alia could feel herself climbing higher...and higher, reaching for something that she desperately wanted to find. To grab hold of.

And then she suddenly reached the crest, and crashed deliciously over the edge into a thick, mistlike oblivion that was warm and honeyed and sweet. It went on for endless, drugging moments, until her body was finally languid and soft, boneless, drenched with lingering, teasing pulses of pleasure, her throat raw from the sharp force of her cries. It took all her strength to force her heavy eyes open, but was worth the effort when she found Rhys's dark face close to hers, his eyes burning with hunger, his expression one of pure, unadulterated need.

She gave him a small, shy smile as he purposefully moved the fingers buried deep inside her, stroking them lightly against her sensitive inner tissues, as if he wanted to remind her of where he was...of what he'd done. That he was penetrating her. That he'd made her come apart in his arms with nothing more than a touch. And then he was pulling his fingers from her tight hold, his voice a dark, velvety rasp as he said, "I wonder if you taste as good as you feel."

With wide eyes, Alia watched him lift his hand to his lips, taking the two glistening fingers inside his mouth. A deep moan rumbled in his chest, as if he was swallowing pleasure, and then he pulled the digits free, staring down at her with an awed, arrested expression. "I've never done that before," he admitted in a deep voice that reminded her of a rich, burnished brandy.

She wet her bottom lip with her tongue, still dazed by the lingering pulses of bliss that rolled through her, languid and warm and rich. "Done what?"

He pressed his hips against hers, letting her feel the shocking size of his hardened shaft, and placed his warm hand against the side of her throat, stroking the tender skin beneath her chin with his callused thumb. "Made a woman reach her peak with nothing more than my fingers. Or put her taste in my mouth."

Her eyes went round. She would have thought a worldly man like Rhys would have already experienced everything there was sexually. "You haven't?"

He gave her a wry, tender smile. "The women I've taken to bed have only been interested in my—" He suddenly cut himself off, the faintest tinge of pink warming his cheekbones, and she realized he was blushing. She could well imagine what he'd been about to say. The massive ridge of his erection was still lodged heavily against her softly pulsing core, her body desperate for the feel of him inside of her. And yet she wanted more than his magnificent body. She wanted, in a word, *everything*.

Pushing his damp hair back from his brow, she murmured, "Well, I'm interested in *all* of you. In fact,

I think I could become quite addicted to having your hands on me."

"Christ, don't say that," he said raggedly, his body flinching in reaction.

"Why?" she asked. "It's true. When you touch me I lose my mind. I lose everything, until there's nothing but you and the way you make me feel. Is it always like this between lovers?"

He shook his head, starting to pull away, his expression grim, but she refused to let him go, digging her fingers into his hard biceps. Though he could have easily broken her hold, he cursed and lowered his body back against hers, instantly taking her mouth in another deep, eating kiss. He kissed her until she couldn't remember her name...until she'd forgotten what it was like to breathe...to not have his mouth on hers. When he finally broke away, she pulled in huge lungfuls of air, her eyes squeezed tight against the burning rush of tears. Her neck arched as he kissed his way down her throat, his big hand pushing its way back between her legs.

"You're so goddamn beautiful," he rasped, kissing a damp path across her bared shoulder, while his fingers teased her tender, swollen opening. She shivered, and he suddenly pressed three fingers inside the tight entrance at the same time he closed his teeth on the sensitive cord between her shoulder and neck. He growled as he bit down hard enough to leave a mark, the thick penetration of his fingers and the aggressive hold of his mouth shoving her into another hard, pulsing burst of pleasure. She cried out again, the keening sound echoing sharply off the rocky walls of the cave until it sounded like a thousand voices screaming out in ecstasy.

The blissful, addictive explosion of heat that fired through her body scared her with its intensity, and Alia knew, in that moment, that she was capable of taking this too far without making her confession. And no matter how badly she wanted it, she *couldn't* do that to Rhys.

"Sorry," he whispered in a low, aching rasp as he pressed his lips to the burning mark on her shoulder. He kissed the reddened skin, then dragged his mouth against her flesh as he made his way back to her mouth. He gentled her with a deep, hungry kiss that coursed through her like a warm, intoxicating wine. He said so much with the touch of his mouth against hers—without using a single word—and she felt the burn of tears rush up from the depths of her soul. She could taste herself on his lips…his tongue, the startling intimacy breaking her open, like something fragile and vulnerable that had no defenses. *I love him*, she thought, knowing it was irrevocably true. Loved him in ways that she couldn't even put words to, they were so precious and tender and soft.

He lifted a few inches away to stare down at her, his gaze piercing, fingers long and thick within her body, barely moving as they continued to gently thrust within her. "Are you bewitching me, Alia? Using your magic on me?"

"No," she whispered, shaking her head. "I…thought about it, but could never bring myself to do it. It would be wrong. A violation of your…heart. I could never do that to you, Rhys."

He studied her face, touching upon each feature with his smoldering gaze, and she could tell the instant he decided to believe her. "I know I need to leave you alone, but I can't stop. Not yet," he groaned, touching her deeper. "I want to put my mouth on you, first. Touch you with my tongue."

The rough, huskily spoken words made her shiver. Made her long to surrender. But she'd made a promise to herself. One that she knew she had to keep, no matter how badly she wanted to simply give in and lose herself to the beauty of his possession.

Staring into his beautiful eyes, she asked the one

question that could change the path of her future. "Do you care about me, Rhys?"

His gaze slid away, his expression instantly tightening with what looked like an angry regret as he took his hand from her body, leaving her cold inside. Empty. "It wouldn't matter if I did, Alia."

"So then you don't?" she pressed, feeling as if her heart was about to shatter into a million pieces.

"It doesn't matter, one way or another," he said heavily, his jaw tight. "I could never make a life with you. It's…impossible."

It was the hardest thing she'd ever done, telling him the truth. "And I can't let this go any further, Rhys. Not if you don't love me."

A hard sound jerked from his grim mouth, like something caught between a bitter laugh and a scornful snarl, and he slowly met her tear-filled gaze, his eyes burning fiercely with heat. The silvery gray was liquid and bright with unmistakable warning. "Trust me, Alia," he said softly. "You don't want me to love you."

"Then we have to stop." Gritting her teeth, she fought for the strength to push him away, the solid muscles of his chest hard and firm beneath her hands. He was too strong and heavy for her to physically move, but he followed her cue and climbed to his feet.

Shifting into a sitting position, she opened her mouth as she pulled her skirt over her knees, but before she could say anything, he cut her off, saying, "There's no need for an explanation. You did the smart thing."

She couldn't stop the trembling of her mouth…her body. "I w-wish you'd let me explain."

"What's to explain?" he rasped, pulling one hand down his face, his gaze focused intently on some distant patch of ground, as if he was being careful *not* to look at her. "You were right to stop this, Alia. More so than you even realize. There are things about the Charteris that most outsiders don't know. Important things."

"Like what?" she whispered.

Like what? Such an innocent question, and yet Rhys hated to have to give her an answer.

Scraping his roughened palm over his jaw, he suddenly thought of how she'd called him beautiful. Such a strange thing for him to remember, when he knew he was anything but. Of all the adjectives that could be used to describe him, beauty wasn't one of them. At several inches over six feet and packed with hard, powerful muscle, he was accustomed to inspiring fear in people. Women tended to be interested in him only as a sort of challenge—as if they enjoyed risking intimacy with a wild, dangerous creature. They didn't see him as a thing of beauty—they simply saw him as a *thing*.

And now Alia would think the same. He took a moment to savor the way she'd looked at him before, her blue eyes soft and sweet and full of longing, then forced himself to tell her the truth.

6

"There's a kind of physiological transformation that happens when we have sex with someone we…care about," Rhy explained, "which can be deadly if the woman isn't of Charteris blood. If she's someone who inspires strong emotion within us, but whose body is vulnerable. There are many who believe that it was meant to ensure we only bred within the clan, keeping the species pure, since our seed is only fertile during this…period of change. But no one really knows for sure."

Alia worked his confession over in her mind, and began to understand so much that hadn't made sense before. "That's why you said it was surprising that your father hadn't killed your mother in their marriage bed, isn't it? Because she wasn't Charteris." She frowned in confusion as another thought occurred to her. "But you also said that they disliked each other intensely. So then why would it have been dangerous?"

"I've often heard that love and hate are both sides of the same coin," he told her. "I guess I've always thought that with the level of…animosity between them, it might have caused the transformation to take place." And the fact that I was conceived means that my father must have experienced at least some degree of change.

Clearing her throat, she quietly asked, "What happens, exactly?"

He was silent for a moment, standing with his rigid body turned slightly away from her, his head angled down as he stared intently at some distant point on the ground. "We remain unchanged, so long as we're sharing intercourse with a woman who means nothing to us. But when our emotions are involved, the change takes place and we literally *burn* with heat. Our bodies. Our…seed. Not just warmth, but enough heat to physically burn. To melt your flesh. To have sex with a woman we care about who isn't a Charteris is to kill her." A low, bitter laugh fell from his lips, and he shook his head. "I guess that's why those of us who live away from the clan are all such coldhearted bastards. We know better than to tempt fate."

"So then all this time we've spent dancing around each other," she murmured, "you've kept your distance because you were afraid of hurting me?"

He made a rough sound in his throat, his tall, muscular body vibrating with a powerful tension, hands fisted at his sides. "I already *have* hurt you," he growled, cutting a glittering look toward the juncture between her neck and shoulder, where the impression of his teeth could still be seen. "The heat isn't the only thing that makes us dangerous. We're primal creatures at heart, prone to dominance and aggression. To put it bluntly, Alia, we're rough as hell."

"I might have cried out when you bit me, but I'm not harmed, Rhys. I don't break that easily, or have you forgotten that I'm no more human than you are?"

A strange look crept over his face, darkening his gaze. "You look human enough," he grunted.

"As do many of the ancient clans," she said carefully, "yourself included. But just because I might *look* break-able, doesn't mean that I am. I'll admit that I don't have your incredible size or strength, but I'm not completely without my own resources."

He arched one brow in an arrogant look of disbelief. "Have *you* forgotten your Merrick blood is dormant, Alia?"

A ghost of a smile played at the corner of her mouth. "I'm also half Reavess, Rhys. I'm nowhere near as vulnerable as a human female."

His head tilted a fraction to the side and he took a hesitant step toward her, his expression arrested. "Then why did you stop me? You were…afraid. I could hear the tremor of fear in your voice."

"But not of *you*," she corrected him. "I just… I was afraid of trapping you."

"What does *that* mean?" Rhys grunted with a hard burst of impatience.

She pulled her lower lip through her teeth, her cheeks flushed with heat as she nervously said, "The Reavess don't come into their full powers until we're twenty, which means I'm still a novice in many ways. Still learning… still awakening to the gifts that I've inherited from my mother. But there are aspects of being Reavess that are already a part of me. That's why I stopped you. If we were to… "

He stared, waiting for the words to fall from her lips, when a sound drew his attention. Rhys instantly held up his hand in a wordless command for silence, just as a tall body moved into the mouth of the cave, silhouetted against the darkening morning sunlight, the distant sky going gray with clouds. He couldn't make out the intruder's face, but he knew in an instant who it was, and pain burned through his insides at the knowledge. "Barrett?" he croaked, hoping like hell this didn't mean what he thought it did. What he *knew* it did.

"Thank God I've found you," the soldier called out, lifting his hand in greeting.

Rhys narrowed his eyes. "What the hell are you doing here?"

Barrett's expression turned grim. "I decided to join you last night in Wolcott, but you'd already left by the time I got there. Figuring I might as well stay and enjoy myself, I was still drinking in the tavern when word came around that there were people searching for Alia in the village. I followed them," he explained, his words rough with anger, "and it didn't take long to learn what had happened. Thankfully, I was able to track you from your scent."

Rhys studied his friend across the five or so yards that

separated them, unable to shake the painful knowledge that the soldier was lying. Barrett's dark gaze slid away from the intensity of his stare, and as Rhys drew in a deep breath, the sour stench of Barrett's fear flooded his system. While Rhys's Charteris blood boiled at the thought of his friend's betrayal, it occurred to him that Barrett's words the previous afternoon had been a warning of sorts. That the man had wanted him to go to the village, so that he wouldn't be killed with the others during the attack on Matthew Buchanan. Either that, or Barrett hadn't wanted to pit himself against Rhys's skill with a sword.

God, he'd been so blind. He knew he never should have left Alia and her father in the care of the other guards. That he should have trusted his instincts when he'd felt that something was wrong. He'd made so many mistakes, and now she was going to pay for them all.

"Alia," he said softly, turning his head slightly as he kept his gaze focused on Barrett. "Come here."

She'd been standing a yard or so behind him, but she quickly moved closer. Rhys caught her wrist, positioning her close to his back, her soft breath panting against his shoulder as she peered around his side. He hated that she was afraid. That he'd failed to protect her.

The corner of Barrett's mouth twisted with a pained expression, and he slowly shook his head, a tired, weary sound escaping beneath his breath. "So my secret is out," he said simply, lifting his face to meet Rhys's stare.

"Christ, Barrett, what the hell have you gotten yourself into? You're meant to be one of the good guys."

"We can't all be as saintly as you," Barrett offered in a wry drawl. Rhys could hear the bitterness that flavored his friend's words and wondered why he'd never noticed before. He knew he'd been withdrawing more and more of late, but had he really been that shut down? That blind to what was going on around him?

"If you're in trouble, why didn't you come to me?" he asked, while the wind picked up beyond the cave, thick with the scent of rain, the sky rumbling with a heavy bellow of thunder. "I would have helped you."

"Don't blame yourself, Rhys. There's nothing you could have done to prevent it. The people I'm working for were determined to get to Buchanan one way or another. If not through me, they would have made a deal with one of the others."

He grunted, then said, "There's something I don't understand. If you were helping them, why did they go looking for Alia in the village last night? With your tracking abilities, you would have been able to scent that she hadn't headed toward Wolcott."

"Believe it or not, she just got lucky," Barrett explained with another wry drawl, scrubbing his left hand against his jaw, while his right hand hovered near the hilt of his sword. Though the Consortium guards were trained in the use of *all* weapons, including pistols, they continued to primarily use steel, too often facing things that couldn't be killed with bullets.

"Seems her father was able to put the lie into the crone's mind. I should have realized it was a ruse to throw us off, but I was so distracted worrying that you might come back," Barrett continued, "that you'd return before we were gone, that I didn't pay close enough attention. I…I didn't want you caught in the middle of this, Rhys. I can't tell you how disappointed I was when we finally returned to the cottage and the crone could see that you were with her." Something that looked like regret flickered in Barrett's eyes. "I didn't want you to be a part of it."

"It's not too late. You don't have to go through with this."

"So says our superiors' lauded hero. But we haven't all been as generously rewarded with the Consortium's gold as you have, Rhys. I've enjoyed living beyond my means for too long now, and was forced to make a bad deal," the lanky soldier muttered, his features twisting into a grimace. "One that I can't get out of, even if I wanted to."

Disgust flavored his words as Rhys said, "There's *always* a choice."

"Do you have any idea what these men will do to me?" Barrett snapped, suddenly losing his composure, his face turning ruddy, his eyes wide with panic.

"No more than you deserve," he growled. "Who are you working for? The Collective?"

"No, they're...not human, Rhys. And they're strong— maybe even full-blooded."

"Full-blooded what?" he demanded, casting out the net of his senses, trying to find the scent of others who might have come with Barrett. But the skies had opened up with a light rain, the drizzle falling steadily outside the mouth of the cave, making it impossible to scent anything beyond the entrance.

Barrett shook his head again. "To be honest, I have no idea. But they'll rip me to shreds if I don't give them what they want."

"And what is that?"

Barrett jerked his chin toward Alia, her pale face still peeking around Rhys's shoulder. "The girl is going to show us where her father found the Marker. Then we'll take the rest of them."

"And if we refuse?" he asked, wondering where the others were. Barrett had said "us"—which meant that he wasn't alone.

A low rumble of laughter fell from Barrett's lips as he looked from Alia and back to Rhys's face. "You won't refuse," he said knowingly. "Not when you have something so precious to lose. But I *am* sorry, Rhys. I truly had no choice. I have none now." Barrett began walking forward, and Rhys reacted instantly. In a rapid movement of muscle and primal instinct, he slammed the soldier against the wall of the cave, his right forearm pressed hard against the traitor's throat before Barrett could even draw his sword.

"Damn it, Rhys!" Barrett wheezed, pulling ineffectually at his arm. "These things will kill me if I don't give them what they want. And it won't be an easy death. They'll peel the flesh from my body. Take me apart, piece by piece!"

"I'm going to save them the trouble," he snarled, jamming his arm harder against Barrett's throat.

"Kill me, then," his friend muttered weakly, "but it isn't going to save her. Nothing can save her now."

He heard Alia's suddenly gasp, and as he cut a dark look toward the mouth of the cave, Rhys saw that his suspicions had finally been confirmed.

Just as he'd guessed, the traitor had not come alone.

7

They'd made it to the caves at Wookey Hole in the cool damp of night, the clouds hanging low in the sky, like something pressing in on their bodies, suffocating and thick. The waters of the River Axe that flowed into the cave were freezing, soaking their clothes as they'd traveled into the cavernous depths of the earth, and Alia couldn't stop her teeth from chattering loudly. Or maybe that was simply her reaction to the worry and fear coiling her insides into a dense tangle of knots. Since the moment she'd seen the mental images her father had sent before his death, she'd known the impossible was coming, and was still no closer to understanding how she was going to prevail. If she and Rhys had been alone, they might have devised a means of retrieving the Markers that wasn't going to end in pain and death, but they were surrounded by the enemy.

During the journey, she'd heard Rhys ask Barrett about the other soldiers, and had learned that they were simply mercenaries who'd been hired to help the traitorous guard obtain the crosses. Which meant that the identity of the ones controlling Barrett remained a secret. He had, however, brought the hired soldiers and the old crone along with him, the woman's hunched back and crinkled, gray-tinged skin attesting to her vast age. Still, despite her decrepit appearance, her black eyes were sharp with focus, constantly taking everything in. As she rubbed her gnarled fingers against the cross Alia had been forced to relinquish, the crone watched them with a cold, malicious gaze, the waves of evil rolling off her seeming to fill the dank air of the cave with a rancid stench.

They stood within an alcove nestled in one of the offshoots of the main cavern, the flowing black water of the river at their backs, the wall curving in a half circle before them. The only light came from the flickering lanterns carried by Barrett's men, the golden spill of light casting ominous shadows against the rough, craggy surfaces of stone. There were ten soldiers in all, standing with their backs to the curved perimeter, the ceiling just high enough to clear their heads.

At her side, Rhys vibrated with a cold, deadly rage, the heat from his coiled muscles blasting against her body, though it was unable to dispel the chill of her soggy clothes. They hadn't been able to speak privately, but Alia assumed that he was furious with her for leading Barrett and the others there, to the caves where the Dark Markers were hidden. But she'd had no choice. After his hired swords had arrived, Barrett had threatened to have Rhys killed if she didn't tell them what they wanted to know, which had made the decision an easy one. She'd already lost her father because of these bastards—she wasn't about to lose Rhys, as well. And yet, Alia knew she had merely bought them a small sliver of time. The only reason Rhys was still alive was because the others didn't know if he'd prove useful to them before their task was completed, and she hoped to hell he was coming up with a plan that would get them out of there.

Barrett had already worked his way through the narrow fissure in the center of the alcove's curved wall that led to the small chamber her father had shown her with his mental images. The fissure was protected by a spell so that it wouldn't be detectable to the human eye, but Alia had been able to summon the words that would reveal its location—words her father had shown her before he died. She also knew that in the center of the chamber lay a fiery pit, its orange flames licking into the air like a nest of writhing, hungry serpents. Whoever had hidden the Markers had spelled the pit to continually burn, protecting the valuable treasure that lay at its base. Barrett had already tried several ways to fish the chain-mail bag that contained the Markers from the bottom of the hole, but each of the implements immediately disintegrated when they touched the twisting, magical flames.

As Barrett paced impatiently from one side of the alcove to the other, the crone suddenly rasped, "I can see now that the flames can only be breached by hand."

Barrett cut a furious scowl in her direction. "Then how am I meant to retrieve them without burning my bloody flesh off?"

"Make the girl go," she croaked, her thin lips twisting with a malevolent smile. "Her father must have used one of his wife's spells to retrieve the cross unharmed. He no doubt shared this with the girl."

"That had better be true," Barrett growled as he cut his gaze toward Alia, the sharp edge of panic in his dark eyes impossible to miss. Despite the chill of the cavern air, the soldier was sweating, his normally burnished skin pale in the flickering light of the lanterns. Whoever was pulling his strings, Barrett was clearly terrified of them.

"I can try," Alia said quietly, wincing as Rhys turned his head to glare down at her with a dark look of accusation. Though she was unsurprised by the crone's directive, having expected as much, she hadn't shared her concerns with the man who stood beside her.

"I can't believe you didn't tell me about the fire," he growled in a low, seething voice. "What the hell were you thinking?"

She lifted her shoulders in a slight shrug. "I didn't want to worry you."

"Alia," he groaned, looking as if he wanted to throttle her.

"It will be okay," she whispered, trying to give him a reassuring smile.

Forcing the question out through his clenched teeth, he said, "So you know the spell?"

She tried not to flinch, but Rhys was watching her too closely. "What?" he demanded, missing nothing.

"It's just that my magic isn't powerful enough to work here," she explained, a nervous edge to the words that she couldn't disguise. "This is protected land, guarded by the original powers that set out to protect the Markers."

Rhys's pale gray eyes narrowed with frustration. "Then how did your father manage to obtain the cross?"

"He used one of my mother's spells, like she said." Alia inclined her head toward the crone. "But it's a highly advanced one that I'm not familiar with, which means that it could be...difficult for me."

"Would your father have been able to cast the spell without being Reavess?" he asked, a deep crease settling between the dark slash of his brows.

Alia nodded. "They were truly *joined*, which meant he would have been able to channel my mother's power, even from her *next life*. But as their daughter, my connection only worked while they were alive. I'm sorry, Rhys."

"Don't be sorry," he grunted under his breath, cutting his gaze back toward the others. "It's not as if I would have let you go, anyway."

"She has no choice," Barrett argued loudly, taking a step forward. It was obvious the traitor had been listening to every word of their exchange.

"I'll go in her place," Rhys stated firmly, his deep voice resonating with command.

"What?" she gasped, her jaw dropping with surprise. "No! That's not possible!"

"I'm the best chance you've got," he grunted, his

attention focused completely on Barrett as he held the soldier's panicked stare.

"Please, Rhys! Please don't go in there!" she begged, grabbing hold of his arm.

He turned toward her then, and leaned down to press a tender kiss against her forehead, while his left hand smoothed over the drenched length of her hair. "Don't worry about me," he whispered. "I can do this, Alia. I promise."

"How?" she asked, her voice hitching as he tilted up her chin with the edge of his fist.

The corner of his mouth curved with a grin. "Just because I don't embrace the Charteris part of my blood doesn't mean that I *can't*."

She blinked with surprise. "But you've always done your best to bury that part of yourself, Rhys."

"You're right, because I've always hated it," he replied with a slow nod, his gaze suddenly burning with intensity. "But things are different now. I care about you more than I could ever hate the Charteris."

Tears spilled from her eyes in a hot, salty rush, her throat quivering with emotion. "I don't believe it. You tell me this now, when I'm about to lose you?" she cried, smacking her fists against the solid wall of his chest.

He responded by taking hold of her face in his big

hands and giving her a hard, quick kiss that only made her cry harder. "Don't be scared," he murmured, pressing his forehead against hers. "I'll get you out of this alive, Alia. I promise."

"You're the one I'm worried about," she said brokenly. "*You*, Rhys. Not me."

He kissed her again, so gently that it was almost a physical pain in her heart, and then he pulled away. "Keep her here," he grunted, staring at Barrett as he turned his back on her. "And I'll get you the bloody crosses."

Doing his best to ignore the wrenching sound of Alia's crying, Rhys carefully made his way through the narrow fissure. Seconds later, he was crouching within the small, domed chamber, its circumference no more than ten feet, staring at the shallow pit dug into the middle of the floor. Fire licked from the hole like a dragon's fiery breath, and the corner of his mouth twitched with bitter humor.

"Fitting," he muttered, before pulling his shirt over his head and dropping it onto the stone floor of the chamber. He knelt beside the pit, his gaze focused intently on the angry, licking flames. They looked like tongues of fire that were eager for a taste of his flesh, but he wasn't afraid. No, his only fear was for Alia's safety. With a deep breath, Rhys fisted his right hand and closed his eyes, concentrating on calling up the primal blood of the ancient beast that dwelled within him. When he felt the searing change ripple beneath his skin, he leaned forward and reached deep into the hole.

As his fingers grazed the rough surface of the bag that lay on the bottom, Rhys let out a shaky breath of relief and opened his eyes. He'd expected at least a twinge of hot, fiery pain, but instead, the flames lapped against his arm like something chilly and damp, making him shiver. Though he remained in his human shape, he'd managed to partially transform his entire arm, his skin now gleaming with a deep, burnished sheen that was capable of resisting the fire's eating flames. Surprisingly, his arm looked much the same, but for the golden, blinding glow that he'd only ever seen in the scales of a Charteris when they'd fully shifted into their dragon form.

Hating that Alia was left back in the cave without him, Rhys quickly fisted his hand around the top of the chain-mail bag and pulled it free. A swift look within the bag showed a glittering tangle of ornate crosses, their thick arms overlapping one another, all of them jumbled together so that it was impossible to tell how many there were without dumping them all out, which he didn't have time for. Although he now had the Markers, he still needed a way to get Alia out of there alive. Staring into the flickering light of the flames, Rhys thought of the stories he'd heard of Charteris warriors who could hold fire…and control it. Would it be possible for him to do the same? He had no idea, but he was ready to try.

With his mind made up, he held the bag in his left hand and thrust his right back into the flickering flames of the fire. When he made his way back out to the others only moments later, Barrett's eyes gleamed with an unholy light as he eyed the bag still clutched within Rhys's left hand.

"Is that them?" the soldier croaked, his voice weak with relief.

Rhys nodded in response as he kept moving nearer to Alia. He was sure Barrett or one of the others would have stopped him if they'd been paying attention, but each of their greed-filled gazes remained locked on the bag that swung from his fist.

"Give them to me," Barrett suddenly snarled, his right hand resting on the hilt of his sword. "Don't try anything stupid, Rhys, or I swear she'll pay."

Like hell she will, he thought, stepping sideways to

close the distance between them until she stood no more than a foot away, her back to the dark waters of the river.

"Alia," he said softly, cutting a swift look at her tear-drenched face. "I just wanted you to know that I love you."

And then, after taking a deep breath, Rhys shoved her into the river.

The instant she hit the water, he looked back toward the others and opened his right hand, revealing the burning ball of fire that flickered and danced there, hovering upon his palm. The crone cried out, obviously seeing what he meant to do, but it was already too late. Barrett and the hired soldiers rushed toward him, their swords raised, but Rhys was too quick. Allowing the change to ripple over the entire surface of his body, he threw his arm up into the air, and the fireball exploded in a stunning eruption that swept through the alcove. The night filled with the horrific sound of tortured screaming, the men burning beneath the roaring fury of the flames.

Only the crone remained standing, her hunched body blistering as the vicious blaze consumed her. She cackled a shrill burst of laughter, and managed to raise her burning arms, the skin melting away, revealing bits of bone beneath. Rhys cursed under his breath as he realized she intended to take her revenge before a fiery death consumed her. He closed his eyes, emptying his mind of everything but Alia, and prayed that she'd had the sense to swim to safety. Then a violent blast of power flew from the crone's dying body and slammed into him. He hit the ground, hard, his body engulfed in a massive cloud of sizzling flames.

8

Alia was preparing to push up from the bottom of the river, when she saw the fiery explosion lash out over the rippling surface of the water, her mind screaming with terror for Rhys's safety. The second the blazing orange glow of the flames began to fade, she broke through the water's surface with a hard gasp. The thick, nauseating smell of burnt flesh in the air made her gag, but she fought the reflex, her panicked gaze finding Rhys's glowing body just as the crone slammed him with a wall of molten flame and he crashed to the ground. In that instant, Alia found herself filled with the most savage need to protect that she could have ever imagined. It was a roaring firestorm in her veins—unstoppable and pure—fueled entirely by love.

Chanting the ancient words of a dangerous incantation that only the most learned Reavess witches should have been capable of completing, Alia called on the powerful blood of her ancestors and forced everything she had into the spell. Power surged through her, punching against her insides, building and building, until it suddenly burst free in a raging wave of energy, forcing the waters of the river to rise up high into the air. The towering wall of water hovered there for a single instant, shimmering and dark, and then it crashed over Rhys's body, extinguishing the flames, while at the same time it slammed the crone viciously into the wall of the cave. Her charred body exploded on impact, disintegrating into blackened pieces of ash that scattered through the air before floating slowly down to the wet ground.

Climbing clumsily from the banks of the river, Alia slipped three times in her haste to reach Rhys, and then she was finally kneeling beside his stunningly naked body—his clothes destroyed by the flames—with her hands pressed urgently against the lingering heat in his face, the stubble that darkened his jaw rough against her palms.

"Rhys, wake up!" she cried, gently shaking him. Three of the lanterns had miraculously managed to remain lit, illuminating the dark beauty of his face, his skin somehow unharmed, as if the flames of the fire had never touched him. He no longer glowed with that blinding, golden light that she'd seen, and so she shook him harder, nearly crying out with relief when his eyelids flickered open, his gray gaze locking instantly with hers.

"What happened?" he growled, quickly sitting up, his expression one of deadly intent as he looked around the alcove, ready to protect her.

When he realized the others were all dead and looked back at her, Alia gave him a wobbly smile, her eyes glassy with tears. "It looked as if you might get yourself killed trying to save me, and I wasn't willing to let that happen."

His own eyes went wide. "You saved me from the crone?"

"I guess we saved each other," she whispered, then slowly shook her head. "Although, I didn't really save you, I guess, so much as woke you up, since the fire doesn't seem to have hurt you at all. Her blast of power must have just knocked you out. But when I saw what she was doing to you, I ordered the river to slam her into the wall and she disintegrated." The corner of her mouth twitched as she added, "I seem to be pretty protective where you're concerned."

"Just promise me that you won't ever do anything that dangerous again," he grunted, looking as if he was caught in her gaze, unable to look away. "Because I couldn't live if I lost you, Alia."

She smoothed his hair back with her fingertips, somehow finding the strength not to ogle his naked body, though it wasn't easy, seeing as how the man was pure, mouthwatering perfection. Hoping he could see the truth of her words in her eyes, she said, "It's the same for me, Rhys."

He quietly said her name, just before he gave her a dazzling smile that made her breath catch.

"I still can't believe everything that's happened. What you did was so amazing," she said with a watery laugh, smiling back at him. "What you did...I've never seen anything like that in my entire life."

"Seems a Charteris's skin is more useful than I would have ever imagined," he offered in a wry drawl.

"Can you show me?" she asked. "I wasn't able to see that clearly from the river."

He lifted his arm in answer to her question, and as she watched, the dark skin of his forearm began to glimmer and shine again with a deep golden glow. "It's beautiful," she whispered, carefully stroking the luminous skin with her fingertips.

An endearingly lopsided grin tipped the corner of his mouth. "And, thankfully, completely fireproof."

She laughed again, staring into his eyes. "You look so happy," she said softly, unable to look away from the breathtaking beauty of his expression.

"That's because I *am* happy," he told her, cupping his palm against the side of her face. "God, Alia, I thought I was going to lose you."

"Oh, Rhys. How could I die when the man I love just told me that he loves me, too?"

"You really didn't know?" he asked, the words rough with emotion.

Another shivery burst of laughter fell from her lips. "I had no idea!"

There was a certain fire in his eyes as he watched her, the pale gray changing, becoming something that looked liquid and hot. Pure silver that'd been melted down, shimmering and bright, and achingly beautiful. "How is that even possible?" he wondered, his voice a deep, decadent assault on her senses. "I would have thought I was so obvious, seeing as how I spend my every waking moment thinking about you. Wondering what you're doing, what you're thinking, what you're feeling. And then, instead of finding oblivion in sleep, you're there as well, tormenting me, tempting me to take things I thought I could never have. You've driven me out of my mind with need, Alia. How could you *not* know? Are you blind?" he demanded, his tone suddenly cut with an endearing note of exasperation. "I thought the Reavess were supposed to be perceptive!"

"We are," she whispered. "But we're often blind to the things we want most to see, allowing our desires and emotions to cloud our vision."

His expression pulled tight with pain as he said, "I want you so badly it's killing me, but it would be so easy for me to hurt you. Even if you are stronger than a human, I could...I could still burn you, Alia."

"But you won't," she assured him, wondering if her grin looked as smug as it felt. "And I'll tell you why. Because Reavess witches can assume the traits of their mates during *joining.* Which means that you can't hurt me, Rhys, no matter how *hot* you become."

"Are you serious?" he rasped, so still he looked as though he wasn't even breathing.

She nodded, then bit the corner of her lip, knowing there was more that she had to tell him. "But I'm afraid I have another confession," she said huskily. "There's something else about the Reavess witches that no one outside of the bloodline and their husbands know."

"And what's that?"

"When a Reavess mates with the man who holds her heart," she told him, "it links him to her, body and soul, in an unbreakable bond that can never be undone. I know it sounds incredible, but it's true. If we make love, it will bind you to me forever."

For a moment, his shock made his face go blank, wiping it clean of expression. And then he started to laugh, the rumbling sound sexy and low, the expression on his face so beautiful, it hurt just to look at him. *"That's* why you pushed me away this morning?"

She nodded, heat blooming beneath her skin, burning in her cheeks. "I didn't know if you loved me, and I didn't want to trap you, binding you forever to a woman you didn't care about. Even if she *was* me."

"You silly, beautiful girl," he groaned, pressing his

lips to her forehead. "You can't trap something that's already yours."

Her pulse raced at his words, roaring in her ears, but she had to be certain that there were no misunderstandings. "Are you sure?" she asked. "Because once done, it's not something that can be *undone*. You'll be stuck with me for the rest of your life, Rhys."

"And in the *next life*, too. Right?"

She nodded, staring deeply into his eyes, as if she could find the proof of his honesty there. He rubbed his thumb across the curve of her cheekbone, the smoldering, joyful look burning there in his gaze, making her heart pound…her body melt. "And what will happen when you bond us together?" he asked with another easy, lopsided grin while moving to his feet in a devastating display of muscle and long, masculine lines that damn near made her hyperventilate.

She swallowed, blinking, struggling to get her voice past the shivering knot of emotion in her throat. "Well, for one thing," she finally managed to rasp, "we'll be able to communicate with our minds. And our children will be able to communicate with us, too."

"Children," Rhys murmured as he reached down and pulled her to her feet, pressing her against the heavy beat of his heart. The idea of having a family with Alia was so beautiful and exciting, he could barely contain himself. "I like the sound of that."

Slipping the Marker her father had found into the chain-mail bag with the others, Rhys held the bag tight as he lifted Alia into his arms. Staring into her luminous eyes, he said, "Now, let's get out of here, so that you can show me exactly what this *joining* will be like."

Cradling her against his chest, he carried her out of the smoky cave, into the milky moonlight. The night was quiet, the storms moving away into the distance, and he took a deep breath, filled with a strange sense of grace and light and beauty, as if his life had somehow been touched by a miracle. One that he was holding possessively in his arms.

"Where are we going?" she asked, after he'd borrowed some clothes from one of the packs the hired soldiers had tied to their horses and was settling her atop his stallion.

Rhys wondered if his smile looked as wolfish as it felt. "We'll put a little distance between us and this place, just in case anyone comes looking for Barrett tonight. And then we're going to find the nearest inn that we can."

"You must be exhausted," she murmured as he settled his big body behind hers.

"Not in the slightest," he rasped in her ear, wondering if she had any idea how badly he needed her.

They rode hard for a few hours, until Rhys knew he was running the risk of stopping, laying her down on the ground and taking her right there. When they came to the next village, he headed straight for the first inn he could find. By the time they'd made it up to their room, they were both panting with anticipation. He all but dragged her into the warm, firelit room, before quickly slamming the door and bolting it shut.

Then he turned toward her, and tried to remind myself that he needed to take it slow, before he scared her away, when all he wanted was to be inside of her—a part of her—as quickly as possible.

Alia watched as Rhys's face tightened with a hard, predatory look of desire, before he took a deep breath and set the Markers down on the low chest beside the door. She stared at the chain-mail bag. "Are you sure this is what you want, Rhys?" she asked as she stared at the chain-mail bag." My life won't be easy. I'll have to protect the Markers. Keep them from falling into the wrong hands." She forced herself to look back at him, her mouth trembling as she said, "If you come with me, you'll be turning your back on everything. On everyone."

He walked to her, towering over her as he gently took her face in his large hands, his heavy-lidded gaze locked with hers. "There *is* no one but you, Alia."

"Rhys," she said breathlessly, fully aware of his intent. "We haven't even bathed yet. I must look awful."

"You're the most beautiful woman I have ever seen, and I've wanted you for five long months that have felt like excruciating years," he growled, ripping at the buttons of her gown. "I'm sorry, but I can't wait any longer."

She could feel his desperation, his need, in the shuddering of his body, the tremor of his muscles. His hands were everywhere, stroking…touching, stripping her of her clothes. She didn't know how he'd manage to remove his own as well, her head dizzy from his dark, devastating kisses, but suddenly they were falling back on the bed together, his powerful body pressing her into the soft mattress, his skin deliciously hot against hers.

"Spread your legs for me," he groaned. "Let me feel you."

She did as he said, gasping as he pressed between

her thighs, the intimate contact sizzling and sharp. And then she was screaming as he lowered himself down her body and covered the sensitive folds of her sex with his mouth. His tongue was warm and soft as he licked her, a deep, predatory growl of pleasure vibrating against her drenched, tender flesh. He stayed there for what felt like a timeless forever, rubbing…thrusting, doing things to her that were more wonderful and shocking than Alia could have ever imagined. He licked her hungrily, as if she were the most delicious thing he'd ever tasted. As if he could be content for hours to lie there between her thighs for hours. She trembled and twisted and screamed as the first orgasm tore through her, and he growled louder as he pressed his face tighter against her, his tongue alternately thrusting inside her and lapping eagerly against the softly pulsing heat of her clit.

As she gasped again for breath, Rhys moved back over her, suckling gently on both her nipples, then moved higher, pushing the damp strands of her hair back from her face. His eyes were bright with emotion as he said, "I never believed in love until I met you. And I know there's still so much for you to show me…for me to learn, but I know that I would give my life to keep you from ever suffering one moment of pain. I know that I can't breathe when you're not with me. And I know that you're the *only* woman I'll ever want."

"Rhys," she breathed out, unable to believe he would make such a heartfelt declaration.

"I know all those things, but most of all, I know that in all the world, you're...you're the most precious, beautiful thing I could have ever imagined." He touched his mouth to hers, shuddering against her, then lifted his head. Staring into her eyes, he said, "I *live* for you, Alia."

Her breath caught with a quiet sob, and it was at that moment that he thrust into her, pushing the heavy, swollen head of his cock inside her. He was too big for the move to be easy, but despite the difficulty, it felt... incredible. The vein-ridged thickness stretching her. The breathtaking hardness and heat. The erotic throbbing of his heartbeat penetrating that most private, delicate part of her.

"Oh, Christ, you're so tight," he growled, carefully pulling back his hips.

"What are you doing?" she panted, panicked, trying desperately to get a hold on his sweat-slick skin so that she could pull him deeper. "Don't leave me!"

"I'm not leaving you," he grunted, his jaw hard as he thrust back in, giving her only slightly more than before. "I'm just trying to be careful."

"Didn't you hear a word I said earlier?" she whispered, cupping the side of his face as she smiled up at him.

"Yes," he forced through his teeth. "But I'm not taking any chances with you."

Alia tilted her head to the side, her long hair tangled across the pillow. "Either touch me as you long to, or don't touch me at all. I won't accept you in half measures, Rhys. I want the *whole* man, not a small part of him."

"That's one of the problems, Alia." He gave a rough, shaky rumble of laughter. "There's nothing *small* about me."

She was sure there was a mischievous light glittering in her eyes as she said, "I know." Her voice was huskier than it'd ever been before, and she saw him stiffen in reaction to the erotic sound. "And I'm not complaining, Rhys. I love everything about you. I love that you're larger than life. I love that there's so…much of you. I want all of it. I *need* all of it. All of *you*."

"I swear there are times you can't be virgin," he said raggedly, shaking his head.

"Why?"

"Because no one so inexperienced should be allowed to be this seductive," he groaned. "It's killing me."

Before she could respond, he suddenly pulled back his hips and thrust into her savagely hard, shoving so deep that she could almost feel him against the pounding beat of her heart. His mouth found hers, possessing her like an erotic fever, his taste primal and wild and completely addictive. She ran her hands down the hot, slick, muscled length of his back, loving the breathtaking power and strength of him as he moved within her, working deeper each time.

"Your eyes," she whispered, sounding awed as she watched the mesmerizing change in color.

The corner of his mouth tipped with a smile. "What about them?"

"The color. They're…gold. Like amber fire."

"I always knew that you worked magic on me," he rumbled in a deep, dark velvety voice, his body slamming into her now in a hard, provocative rhythm that made the headboard slap against the wall with each heavy, aggressive thrust. Lowering his head, his breath was hot in her ear as he said, "You set me on fire, Alia. Every part of you. You're so beautiful…so sweet." He pulled back, the look in his beautiful eyes as he stared down at her melting her down to nothing but pure, raw, mind-shattering need. "And you're mine," he growled. "Always *mine*."

It was mesmerizing, watching the way the glow spread out from his eyes, spilling beneath his skin, until his body was burning like a glittering, incandescent source of light. And just as Alia had told him, her body began to change with his, her skin turning the same mystifying shade of gold. As his skin burned against hers, and inside her body, his massive shaft grew impossibly hotter, thicker, intensifying the pleasure. She writhed beneath him, the sensations surging through her like a devastating wave of pain-edged ecstasy, the ache somehow blending with the screamingly intense pulses of pleasure until she was crying and moaning his name, clawing at him, wanting more…and more. The deep, rhythmic tremors of her building orgasm grew steadily stronger, his powerful body driving into her harder… deeper, and then she exploded, the ecstasy consuming her in a shocking, dizzying explosion of heat and white, blinding light. Her neck arched as she screamed from the brutal, evocative waves crashing through her, each one somehow sweeter and more perfect than the last.

As if consumed by the same violent need that burned through her, Rhys drove himself into her body so hard that the entire bed frame slammed against the wall, the wood cracking sharply just as his own release tore through him, the primal roar that broke from his chest the most delicious sound she'd ever heard. And as he spilled into her, the scorching, shocking blast of heat from his seed pulled a deep, sensual moan from her throat.

Oh, Christ, are you okay? he growled just seconds later, panting for air, and she wondered if he even realized that he'd spoken the words within her mind.

I'm melting with pleasure, she silently whispered, already swept up in another devastating climax that seemed even more powerful than the others. She would have laughed at the breathtaking look of wonder that bloomed over his face, but the intensity of the orgasm swept through her, and she passed out, everything going dark and black and silent. When she finally came back, Rhys's body was plastered against hers, his breath warm against her ear. They stayed like that for a long, endless moment, then finally pulled themselves from the bed so that they could bathe together before the room's crackling fire, in a copper tub of water that steamed from the lingering heat in their bodies. Then they returned to the bed, making love twice more before he wrapped her in his strong arms and pulled her against his chest. They lay on their sides, facing each other, sharing the same pillow…the same air as they breathed, lost in each other's eyes.

"Do you think there's anyone at the Consortium we should tell about the Markers?" she asked, tangling her legs with his.

He shook his head, pulling her closer, as if he wanted nothing more than to absorb her into his body. "Not after what happened with Barrett. There's no one we can trust."

"The danger is still out there," she whispered, "and we still don't know who wants the crosses, or why. But I have an idea that might work for keeping them safe."

"What is it?" he asked, and she had to force herself to concentrate as he shifted back a little to trail his fingertips over her collarbone, before traveling lower, down the center of her chest.

"I was thinking that they should be separated, making them more difficult to find. So we could bury them individually, scattering the locations over as many different countries as we can," she explained, struggling to focus as his fingertips softly circled her navel. "Then we can find some corner of the world that we love more than all the others, and we'll build a home there. One that's filled with laughter and love and as many children as we can fit."

He made a thick sound of excitement in his throat, then kissed her deeply...hungrily, as if he couldn't get enough of her taste. "You know what that means then, don't you?"

"What's that?" she asked breathlessly, still buzzing from his devastating kiss.

"If we're going to have that many babies, then we're going to need lots of practice," he murmured with a wicked smile, rolling her beneath his hard, beautiful body. And moments later, they began to *burn*.

EPILOGUE

Six months later...

Standing at the top of a colorful, flower-covered hill, Rhys stared out over the breathtaking landscape of the Tuscany valley below them. Twilight touched its soft fingers to the majestic beauty of the land, painting it with dappled shades of purple and pink, and yet it was still incomparable to that of the woman at his side, a gentle smile curving her lips as she stared out over the valley with him. Her slender fingers were twined with his, her delicate form pressed close along the left side of his body, as if she couldn't stand to have any space between them. The thought made his pulse quicken, but then it was still a powerful shock to his system, the fact that Alia loved him as desperately as he loved her.

Though they'd learned so much since that harrowing

night at the Wookey Hole Caves, there were still so many questions that remained unanswered. Who had Barrett been working for all those months ago? Why did they want the Markers so badly? What unknown purposes did the crosses possess? And while he and Alia didn't have the answers, they knew, without any doubt, that they were doing the right thing. Especially now that they'd heard fragments of a Gypsy legend that foretold of the return of the Casus—a return that would one day awaken the dormant Merrick bloodlines. Alia was adamant that if that time ever came, their descendants would need a way of finding the ancient crosses, and so they'd decided to leave maps behind that would lead to the Markers' locations.

Now, after months of planning, they'd finally come to the picturesque hillside to bury the first cross. Years from now, after they'd finished hiding the others, they would return to this place and bury the maps alongside the Dark Marker that her father had once taken to study. Alia assured him this cross would be the first to be found, and she planned to spell the maps they would eventually bury here to ensure their preservation. The maps would also be encrypted with a special code that Alia's mother had used for her most powerful spells, making it nearly impossible to break.

"You do realize how difficult we'll have made this for them, don't you?" he'd asked as they'd made their journey to Italy, thinking of the Buchanans who might one day need to find the crosses.

Alia had given him a secret smile as she'd said, "Our bloodline is going to be incredibly powerful. And I'll leave them gifts. Special ones that will help them when the time comes."

Though it seemed an impossible feat, Rhys had no doubt that she would be able to do just that. As her powers grew, it truly awed him, the things she was capable of. But nothing awed him more than the way she'd transformed his life.

Turning his head to gaze down at the precious woman who was now his beloved wife, he murmured, "So you really think they'll be able to find this place?"

She smiled that secret, bewitching smile of hers as they both turned to face each other, her hands settling on his shoulders, while he looped his arms around her waist. "I know they will," she told him, leaning up on her toes to press a tender kiss against his lips. "Just as I know that you're going to make a wonderful father some day, Rhys."

Her words hit him low in his body, then spread outward

in a warm wave of emotion, melting his heart. "How do you know?" he asked, his words soft with reverence.

"Because I know your heart," she murmured, her blue eyes shining with happiness. "I've seen the light inside of you, and it's beautiful."

Rhys's breath caught as he took in her expression. When she looked at him like that, he could almost believe that she truly did see beauty within him.

I love you, he told her, lifting his right hand to cup the side of her face as he stroked his thumb against her soft skin.

Her face tilted a little to the side, into the palm of his hand, and she silently said, *I love you, too. So much, Rhys.*

Thank you, he added, the simple words rough with emotion.

She blinked, and the corner of her mouth lifted with a questioning smile. "For what?"

"For everything," he said in a low voice, pulling her tight against the front of his body. "For coming into my life. For loving me. For showing me what it's like to be happy." His left hand moved between them, covering her belly, where their children would someday grow. "For the family we're going to have one day. For giving me *you*, Alia."

Tears slipped onto her cheeks as he kissed his way into her mouth, and he embraced the familiar spill of fire that seared through his veins. He no longer shunned the heat. How could he, when Alia was his bright, shining light? When he'd first met her, she had been the endless, sunlit sky to his lonely darkness. Then she'd made him a part of her world, and brought the warmth of the sun to his cold existence. She had brought him laughter and love and smiles, as well as a sweet, joyful hope for the future.

She had brought him pure, breathtaking happiness, and in return, Rhys loved her more than any man had ever loved a woman.

He always would.

Forever.

* * * * *

Don't miss

TOUCH OF TEMPTATION
by Rhyannon Byrd.

Available next month in Nocturne™!

A Goddess of Partholon Novel

When an antique vase calls to her while on holiday,
Shannon Parker finds herself transported to
Partholon, where she's treated like a goddess.

But it also comes with a ritual marriage to a centaur
and threats against her new people. Can Shannon
survive this new world and ever find her way home?

www.mirabooks.co.uk